LONG WAY DOWN

To Fargo's left was an erosion-worn gully that split the slope from bottom to top. All he had to do was make it there without being spotted. Tensing, he waited for the right moment. It came a few seconds later when one of the Apaches went over to Sissy One and said something Fargo couldn't quite catch. The other Apache was watching them.

His elbows and knees pumping, Fargo crawled toward the gully. He braced for an outcry or a shot, but none came. Pleased at how easy it had been, he slid over the top. He was halfway to the bottom when he realized he didn't have the gully to himself.

Coiled at the bottom was one of the biggest rattlesnakes Fargo had ever seen, and he was sliding straight toward it. . . .

TEXAS TRIGGERS

by

Jon Sharpe

SIGNET
Published by New American Library, a division of
Penguin Group (USA) Inc., 375 Hudson Street,
New York, New York 10014, USA
Penguin Group (Canada), 90 Eglinton Avenue East, Suite 700, Toronto,
Ontario M4P 2Y3, Canada (a division of Pearson Penguin Canada Inc.)
Penguin Books Ltd., 80 Strand, London WC2R 0RL, England
Penguin Ireland, 25 St. Stephen's Green, Dublin 2,
Ireland (a division of Penguin Books Ltd.)
Penguin Group (Australia), 250 Camberwell Road, Camberwell, Victoria 3124,
Australia (a division of Pearson Australia Group Pty. Ltd.)
Penguin Books India Pvt. Ltd., 11 Community Centre, Panchsheel Park,
New Delhi - 110 017, India
Penguin Group (NZ), 67 Apollo Drive, Rosedale, North Shore 0632,
New Zealand (a division of Pearson New Zealand Ltd.)
Penguin Books (South Africa) (Pty.) Ltd., 24 Sturdee Avenue,
Rosebank, Johannesburg 2196, South Africa

Penguin Books Ltd., Registered Offices:
80 Strand, London WC2R 0RL, England

First published by Signet, an imprint of New American Library,
a division of Penguin Group (USA) Inc.

First Printing, February 2009
10 9 8 7 6 5 4 3 2 1

The first chapter of this book previously appeared in *Idaho Gold Fever*, the
three hundred twenty-seventh volume in this series.

Copyright © Penguin Group (USA) Inc., 2009
All rights reserved

REGISTERED TRADEMARK—MARCA REGISTRADA

Printed in the United States of America

Without limiting the rights under copyright reserved above, no part of this publication may be reproduced, stored in or introduced into a retrieval system, or transmitted, in any form, or by any means (electronic, mechanical, photocopying, recording, or otherwise), without the prior written permission of both the copyright owner and the above publisher of this book.

PUBLISHER'S NOTE
This is a work of fiction. Names, characters, places, and incidents either are the product of the author's imagination or are used fictitiously, and any resemblance to actual persons, living or dead, business establishments, events, or locales is entirely coincidental.

The publisher does not have any control over and does not assume any responsibility for author or third-party Web sites or their content.

If you purchased this book without a cover you should be aware that this book is stolen property. It was reported as "unsold and destroyed" to the publisher and neither the author nor the publisher has received any payment for this "stripped book."

The scanning, uploading, and distribution of this book via the Internet or via any other means without the permission of the publisher is illegal and punishable by law. Please purchase only authorized electronic editions, and do not participate in or encourage electronic piracy of copyrighted materials. Your support of the author's rights is appreciated.

The Trailsman

Beginnings . . . they bend the tree and they mark the man. Skye Fargo was born when he was eighteen. Terror was his midwife, vengeance his first cry. Killing spawned Skye Fargo, ruthless, cold-blooded murder. Out of the acrid smoke of gunpowder still hanging in the air, he rose, cried out a promise never forgotten.

The Trailsman they began to call him all across the West: searcher, scout, hunter, the man who could see where others only looked, his skills for hire but not his soul, the man who lived each day to the fullest, yet trailed each tomorrow. Skye Fargo, the Trailsman, the seeker who could take the wildness of a land and the wanting of a woman and make them his own.

The hard land west of the Pecos, 1861—where the Apache reigned, and the unwary paid for their follies in pain and blood.

1

The sun was killing him.

It hung at its zenith, a blazing yellow furnace. For weeks now, west Texas had been scorched by relentless heat. The land baked; the vegetation withered; the wildlife suffered. It was the worst summer anyone could remember in the desert country west of the Pecos River.

That included Skye Fargo. He had been through Texas before, plenty of times, and he had never experienced heat like this. Heat so hot, his skin felt as if it were on fire. With each breath, he inhaled flame into his lungs. Squinting up at the cause, Fargo summed up his sentiments with a single, bitter, "Damn."

His horse was suffering, too. The Ovaro was as good a mount as a man could ask for. It had stamina to spare, but the merciless heat had boiled its strength away to where the stallion plodded along with its head hung low, so weary and worn that Fargo had commenced to worry. Which was why he was walking and leading the stallion by the reins.

Any man stranded afoot in that country had one foot in the grave. Any man except an Apache.

The Mescaleros had roamed that region since anyone could remember. Tempered by the forge of adversity, they prowled in search of prey. The heat didn't affect their iron constitutions. And, too, they knew all the secret water holes and tanks. They thrived where most whites would perish.

Most, but not all. The harsh land of cactus, mesquite

and limestone rock was home to scattered settlers. Isolated valleys amid the maze of canyons and plateaus were pockets of green against the backdrop of brown. But not this summer. Now most of those green valleys were as brown as everything else.

It was just Fargo's luck to be passing through after delivering a dispatch to Fort Davis. He was on his own, and headed for cooler climes. The sun, though, was doing its best to roast him and the Ovaro alive, and it was close to succeeding.

Fargo stopped and gazed out over the bleak, blistered landscape. He licked his cracked lips. Or tried to. His mouth was as dry as the rest of him, and he had no spit to spare. He glanced back at the Ovaro. "Hold on, boy. I'll find us water if it's the last thing I do."

It might well be.

Broad of shoulder and narrow of waist, Skye Fargo was all muscle and whipcord. He wore buckskins and boots and a white hat made brown by dust. Around his neck was a splash of color: a red bandanna. At his hip hung a Colt. In an ankle sheath inside his boot was an Arkansas toothpick. From the saddle jutted the stock of a Henry rifle.

At first glance, Fargo looked no different from most frontiersmen. But he had more experience in the wild than any ten of them put together. In his travels he had been most everywhere, seen most everything. He'd lived with Indians and knew their ways. In short, if any white could make it through that country, Fargo could.

Or so he thought when he started out. Now he wasn't so sure.

Fargo tried to swallow, and couldn't. He ran a hand across his hot brow and was surprised at how little sweat there was. He had little moisture left in him. His body was a cloth wrung dry, and unless he found water, and found it soon, his bleached bones would join the many skeletons that already littered the desert.

Fargo had to force his legs to move. A bad sign, that.

His body was giving out. The steely sinews that had served him in such good stead had turned traitor and would not do as he wanted unless he lashed them with the whip of his will.

The Ovaro went a short way and abruptly stopped.

Fargo tugged on the reins to keep the pinto moving, but it didn't respond. He turned and saw that it had its head up and its ears pricked, and it was staring fixedly to one side. He looked and saw nothing but boulders and dirt and a few brown bushes and tufts of brown grass.

"There's nothing there. Come on." Fargo gave another tug and the Ovaro plodded after him, but it kept staring and its nostrils flared.

Belatedly, Fargo's heat-dulled mind realized that something was out there. Or, more likely, *someone.* No animal would be abroad in that heat. And since there wasn't another white within miles, so far as Fargo knew, that left the last ones Fargo wanted to meet up with.

That left the Mescalero Apaches.

Fargo was in no shape for a fight. Alert now, he watched from under his hat brim but saw nothing to account for the Ovaro's interest. He was about convinced the stallion was mistaken when a hint of movement sent a tingle of alarm down his spine.

He was being stalked.

Outwardly, Fargo stayed calm. He mustn't let on that he knew. He kept on walking, his right arm at his side, his hand brushing his Colt. It would help if he had some idea how many were shadowing him, but that was like counting ghosts. Fargo wondered why they hadn't attacked yet. It could be they were waiting for the heat to weaken him even more. Or maybe there was a spot up ahead better fitted for an ambush.

Ordinarily, Fargo would have swung onto the Ovaro and used his spurs. But the stallion was in no shape for a hard ride. He doubted it would last half a mile without collapsing. And then the Apaches would have him.

Fargo racked his brain. His best bet was to lure them in close where he could drop them with his Colt. But Apaches weren't stupid. They wouldn't fall for whatever trick he tried unless it was convincing.

Then it hit him. The answer was in the sky above. He squinted up at the sun again, and made a show of running his sleeve across his face. He wanted the Apaches to think he was about done in. True, he was, but he still had a spark of vitality left, and that spark might save his hide.

Before him, the country flattened. In the distance were some hills.

Fargo stopped and gazed idly about, then moved toward a large cactus. It offered hardly any shade, but he plopped down in what shade there was and sat with his head hung and his shoulders slumped to give the impression he just couldn't go on.

Other than cacti, the spot Fargo had chosen was open. No one, not even a wily Apache, could get at him without him seeing. They might come in a rush but only after he collapsed. And that's exactly what he did. He put his left hand under him as if he were so weak he could barely sit up. He stayed like that awhile, then let his elbow bend and slowly sank onto his side. From where he lay he could see his back trail but not much to either side. He could see the Ovaro, though, and that was what counted.

For the longest while, nothing happened.

The heat seeped into Fargo's bones, into his very marrow. He began to feel sleepy and almost gave a toss of his head to shake the lethargy off. But that would give him away. Struggling to keep his senses sharp, he saw the Ovaro lift its head and stare to the north. Fargo shifted his gaze in that direction but his hat brim hid whatever was out there.

Fargo seldom felt so vulnerable, so exposed. He slowly shifted his cheek so he could see past the brim. All he saw were cacti. Yet the Ovaro was still staring.

Where were they? Fargo wondered. Apaches were masters at blending in. They could literally hide in plain sight. Once, years ago, he met an Apache scout who showed him how. They had been standing in open country, and the Apache had him turn his back and count to ten. When he turned around, the man was gone. Fargo had been stumped and called out to him, and the Apache, grinning, rose from behind a bush no bigger than a breadbasket where he had dug a shallow hole and covered himself, all in the blink of an eye.

Damned impressive, that little demonstration.

Fargo searched the vicinity but saw nothing. He looked so long and so hard that his eyes started to smart. He decided to watch the Ovaro instead, thinking the stallion would react once the warriors were close enough. It wasn't staring to the north anymore. It was staring at something *behind* him.

Fargo's skin crawled. At any moment he might get an arrow or a knife in the back. He was sorely tempted to roll over, but if he did, the warrior would melt away.

It was a nightmare, lying there waiting for something to happen. Fargo's nerves jangled like a shriek of fire in a theater. The taut seconds stretched into a minute and the minute into two, and it was a wonder he didn't snap and leap to his feet.

Then the Ovaro nickered and stamped a heavy hoof.

Fargo rolled over, drawing the Colt as he moved. It was safe to say the Apache a few feet away with a knife in hand was considerably surprised, but he recovered quickly. The bronzed warrior sprang, the steel of his blade glinting in the sunlight.

Flat on his back, Fargo fanned the Colt twice. At that range he could hardly miss. Both slugs caught the Apache high in the chest and twisted him half around. Baring his teeth, he got a hand under him and levered forward, seeking to bury his knife with his dying breath. The tip was inches from Fargo when the warrior collapsed, sprawling forward on his belly so that his forearm ended up across Fargo. Pushing it off, Fargo heaved erect and spun, braced for an onslaught of war whoops and weapons.

There were no outcries. No other warriors appeared.

Fargo kept turning from side to side. Finally he admitted the obvious. The one he had shot was the only one. With the toe of his boot, he rolled the dead warrior over. The dark eyes were open; they betrayed no shock or fear.

Fargo had no strength to bury him, and no desire to do it even if he had the strength. The man had tried to kill him. Let the buzzards and coyotes gorge. He replaced the spent cartridges, slid the Colt into its holster and patted the Ovaro. "You saved my skin again. Now let's see if I can save us from dying of thirst."

The distant brown hills held little promise. The drought had dried up all the streams, and it was doubtful he would find one flowing.

Fargo's boots were so hot, it felt as if his feet were being cooked. But he refused to give up. It wasn't in him. So long as he had breath he would resist oblivion with all that he was. He liked living too much. He liked to roam the wild places. He liked whiskey. He liked cards and women. He liked women a lot. An hour or two of passion reminded a man why it was good to be alive.

Fargo chuckled, but the sound that came from his parched throat was more like the rattle of seeds in a dry gourd. "God, I need water," he rasped, and it hurt to speak.

The hills grew near. By late afternoon Fargo was among them. And as he had feared, it was more of the same. More endless dry. In all that vast inferno, the only living creatures were the Ovaro and him. Not a single bird was in the air. He had not seen a lizard or snake all day. The scrape of his boots and the thud of the Ovaro's hooves were the only sounds.

Fargo's chin drooped. His blood felt as if it were boiling in his veins. He would gladly find a patch of shade and rest but he honestly didn't know if he could get back up again.

The sun dipped toward the horizon. Once it set, the night would bring welcome relief. But without water it would be fleeting, at best.

His legs leaden, Fargo shuffled grimly on. He nearly lost his hold on the reins when the Ovaro unexpectedly stopped.

"What the hell?"

Turning, Fargo pulled but the Ovaro refused to move. Its head was up and it was staring straight ahead.

Thinking it was another Apache, Fargo spun, his hand dropping to his Colt. But it wasn't a warrior out to do him in.

It was a cow.

Not a longhorn or a steer or a bull but an honest-to-God milk cow, calmly regarding him from fifty feet away while chewing its cud.

Fargo blinked, certain he must be seeing things. "You would think it would be a naked woman."

The cow flicked its ears.

That was when Fargo noticed the tiny bell that dangled from a rawhide cord around its neck. Unless he missed his guess, the cow was a Jersey. He seemed to recollect that the breed got its start on an island of that name somewhere, long ago, but where he picked up that tidbit he had no idea. The kind of cow didn't really matter. It shouldn't be there. And yet it was.

"Pleased to meet you, madam."

The cow went on chewing.

Fargo moved toward it, talking quietly. "Do you live around here? I'd like to meet whoever milks you and ask for some of your milk or some water." Anything to slake his thirst.

Slowly turning, the cow lumbered off along the bottom of a hill. She was thick with flies, and a swish of her tail sent them buzzing.

Fargo followed. He couldn't believe his luck. To have

stumbled on a ranch in the middle of nowhere! Although now that he thought about it, he recollected there were a few hardy souls in those parts. Fools, a lot of folks called them, for daring to put down roots in the heart of Apache territory. No one in their right mind would do such a thing.

The cow was out of sight around the hill.

Anxious to catch up, Fargo stepped into the stirrups. "Sorry," he said to the Ovaro. The stallion apparently smelled or sensed their salvation and needed no urging. It moved before he could tap his spurs. He half feared he would get to the other side of the hill and the cow wouldn't be there, that it really was his overheated mind playing tricks on him.

Then a valley spread before him, a brown valley, a valley as dry as the hills and the desert. And there was the Jersey cow, moving out across a well-worn trail that led to the far end.

Fargo was so intent on the cow that he didn't pay much attention to the hill they had just come around. He realized his mistake when he heard a metallic click. Instinctively, he threw himself from the saddle just as a rifle thundered. He landed on his shoulder and rolled onto his belly. Thinking he had several seconds to locate the shooter, he raised his head. But he was wrong. The rifle boomed again, and yet a third time, and miniature dirt geysers came straight toward his face.

2

Fargo rolled and kept rolling until he collided with a boulder. Scrambling behind it, he palmed his Colt. The shots stopped and quiet fell. Removing his hat, he risked a peek at the Ovaro. The stallion had gone another thirty feet or so and stopped. Too far for him to reach the Henry before the rifleman put a slug or three into him. "Damn," he said under his breath.

The spray of slugs had spooked the cow and it was trotting off. Or as close to a trot as cows ever came.

Fargo scanned the hill. Boulders littered the slope from bottom to top. The shooter could be anywhere. "Damn," he said again. Then, much louder, "Who are you? Why did you shoot at me?"

There was no answer.

"I'm only passing through and need some water. If you have any to spare, I'd be obliged."

The silence mocked him.

Fargo tried a third time. "Can you hear me up there? I don't mean you any harm." When there was no reply, he ducked down and jammed his hat back on. He wasn't about to lie there and wait for the bastard to try again. With all those boulders for cover, he would work his way up the hill and take the fight to the shooter.

His catlike agility and quickness served him in excellent stead, and soon he was hunkered behind a fair-sized boulder partway up the hill. Not one shot had pealed. He began to wonder if maybe the rifleman was gone.

Poking his head out, Fargo focused on a boulder ten

feet higher. Legs churning, he raced toward it. No leaden hornets buzzed him. He dropped to his knees behind the boulder and bent to the left to peer around it. Whoever was up there—if they still were—was well hid. He went to draw back and something hard jammed against the nape of his neck.

Fargo froze.

"This here's a rifle."

Startled by the voice, Fargo started to turn.

"I wouldn't, were I you, mister. I will shoot you if you don't do exactly as I say. Don't think I won't."

Controlling himself, Fargo said, "Didn't you hear me? I'm not out to hurt you."

"You could be lying."

"Do you always greet strangers this way?"

"We have to protect what's ours. Now listen. I want you to get shed of that six-shooter. Nice and slow, or I will blow your head clean off."

"You're awful vicious," Fargo said. But he did as he was told, lowering the Colt close to the ground before dropping it. "Will that do?"

"You did good. When I tell you to, turn around. But not before, you hear?"

"Do you have a name?"

"Doesn't everybody?"

The muzzle was taken from Fargo's neck. He was careful to keep his arms out from his sides and not make any sudden moves.

"You can turn around now," the voice said. "But nice and slow, like before. I'll shoot if you make me."

Complying, Fargo shifted. He was over his initial surprise, and regarded his captor with a mix of amazement and amusement. "You sure do talk tough, girl."

His captor was eleven or twelve, if that. She had stringy brown hair that hadn't been washed in a coon's age and a frayed homespun dress so threadbare it was fit for rags. Her feet were bare and dirty. "I do what I have to, mister. Now hush while I figure out what to do with you."

"Yes, ma'am."

Her face was streaked with grime. Dark eyes, high cheekbones, and an oval chin completed her portrait. She gnawed her lower lip, then said, "I reckon the best thing is to fetch you home to Ma and Pa and let them decide whether you should go on breathing."

"I would like to meet them," Fargo said.

"You might not after Pa gets through with you. He doesn't cotton to outsiders much." The girl's eyes narrowed. "I hope he doesn't beat on you. You sure are a pretty one."

Trying to get on her good side, Fargo said, "Thank you. But it's women who are pretty. You don't call a man that."

"I'll call you anything I want." She stepped back and wagged the rifle. "Head down, pretty man. And no tricks, you hear?"

"What about my revolver?"

"What about it?" she rejoined.

"You're not going to just leave it here, are you?"

"Don't fret. I'll bring it along. Pa might want it for himself." She wagged the rifle again. "Quit stalling and walk."

Fargo felt slightly ridiculous being held at gunpoint by a snip of a girl but he did as she wanted. "You did hear me say all I wanted was some water?"

The girl laughed a strange laugh. "Who doesn't, these days? It's more valuable than gold, Ma says."

Introducing himself, Fargo said over his shoulder, "You haven't told me who you are. The least you could do is be polite and give me you name."

"I suppose it won't hurt. I'm Sissy Three."

"How's that again?"

"Don't your ears work? My name is Sissy Three."

"All right, Sissy. Is that short for sister or—"

"No, no, no," the girl said sharply. "You can't just call me Sissy or you'll get us confused. It's Sissy *Three.* Say it right or don't say it at all."

"Sissy Three? I've never heard a name like that," Fargo admitted.

"And I've never heard of anyone named after the sky before, so we're even, mister."

"How long have you and your family lived out here?"

"You like asking questions, don't you? But we've lived here going on two years now."

"Your folks do know this is Apache country?" Fargo didn't like the idea of children being there.

"Everybody knows that. What a fool thing to ask. You must think we're stupid or something."

"Doesn't it worry you? The Apaches aren't as friendly as I am."

"That's why we're always on our guard. And why I saw you before you saw me. Now hush and walk. When we get to your horse, bring it along."

Fargo didn't mind doing as she wanted, for the time being. Her parents, he reckoned, would be more reasonable. The Jersey cow had stopped running a goodly distance off and was watching them approach. Beyond the cow the valley narrowed. At the end grew a stand of trees. Cottonwoods, their leaves as green as could be, not brown like all the other vegetation. "Why did your family settle in this godforsaken spot, of all places?"

"Didn't you hear me tell you to hush?"

"What difference does it make if we talk? I'm trying to be friendly, is all, girl."

"We didn't pick this spot. It picked us."

"Care to explain?"

"We were heading for Arizona. We have kin there. But our wagon broke—the axle it was—and Pa couldn't fix it. We were short on food and plumb out of water, and then one of my sisters found the spring. So here we are."

"Your accent," Fargo said. "You're from the South?"

"Georgia. The hill country. Which I guess is why people call us hill folk. Pa got into trouble with the law and we had to leave. Ma wasn't too happy about it but she didn't want him behind bars so we sold our place and bought the covered wagon."

"What did your pa do that the law was after him?"

"Mostly he got drunk and beat people up. But one time a man pulled a knife on him and Pa took the knife away and cut him. The law didn't like that. Pa went up before a judge and the judge said that if Pa had one more fight, just one, he would throw Pa in jail and throw away the key."

It all began to make sense, but Fargo had a few questions yet. "Why not go for help? Find someone who can repair your wagon so you can be on your way?" That's what he would do if he was a husband and a father and he was stranded in Apache country.

"Pa wanted to, but Ma wouldn't let him."

"You need to explain that, too."

"Ma likes it here."

Fargo gazed out over the stark, blistered landscape, crawling with Apaches and rattlers, and tried to imagine *any* woman saying such a thing. "Did she fall from the wagon and hit her head when the axle busted?"

Sissy Three laughed. "Her head is fine. She's the thinker in our family. She's smart, my ma."

How smart could she be, Fargo wondered, if she put her family at such risk? But he kept the thought to himself and said instead, "Are you and your sisters happy here?"

It took Sissy Three a while to answer. "No, we're not. It's lonesome, terrible lonesome. But don't you tell my ma I said that. She has her reason for staying, and me and my sisters will help her any way we can."

"I'm looking forward to meeting this family of yours."

"Don't look forward to it too much. Remember what I told you about my pa. He might take it into his head to pound on you."

"I'd pound back."

"You're welcome to try."

"You're not worried I might hurt him?"

Sissy Three laughed again. "Mister, no one can hurt my pa. No one can lick him. He's stronger than you and five men besides. He's never been beat, not in all the fights he's been in."

"There's a first time for everything," Fargo said. But he had no hankering to trade blows with the man, not in the shape he was in.

They were almost to the Jersey cow.

Fargo jerked a thumb at it, asking, "Did this critter come all the way from Georgia with you?"

"Bessie? She sure did. We raised her from a calf. We weren't about to leave her behind."

"Where's the rest of your herd?"

"Bessie is it. She's all we've ever had. All we could afford. She was close to dying when we found the spring. Another couple of days and Ma would have served her for supper."

"Lucky Bessie."

Presently they neared the cottonwoods and Fargo was surprised at how many there were. Several acres, at least. Close to them stood what had to be the most peculiar dwelling he ever came across. Built from boards and cottonwood trunks that had been trimmed of limbs, it looked like something a lunatic might construct. Or someone who was drunk. Part of a dirty sheet hung over an oblong window. The doorway canted at the top so that staring at it gave Fargo the impression *he* must be drunk. The door consisted of several uneven boards with knotholes. Saplings served as crossbeams. The roof was sod, placed haphazardly so that it resembled nothing so much as an overgrown patch of weeds.

"Good God."

"You don't like our house?"

Fargo glanced over his shoulder and grinned. "You've got to admit it's a mite peculiar."

Sissy Three shrugged. "Our cabin back in Georgia wasn't much better. The chinking fell out and in the winter the cold wind blew in and about froze us to death."

"Why didn't your pa fix it?"

"That would take work. And if there's one thing my pa hates, it's work. Ma says he'd lay around doing nothing his whole life long if he could get away with it. She calls him a lazy no-account at least once a day."

"Then why does she stay with him?"

"You'd have to ask her," Sissy Three said, and bobbed her chin.

A woman had come out of the cabin. She had the same brown eyes and high cheekbones and wore a dress as threadbare as her daughter's. She was also barefoot. That was as far as the resemblance went. For where Sissy Three was a snip of a girl, the mother had an hourglass figure and watermelons for breasts—they jutted against her dress as if seeking to burst out. The dress barely fell to the middle of her thighs, exposing creamy skin bronzed by the sun. "Well, what do we have here?" she asked in a husky voice that sent a tingle clear down to Fargo's toes.

"He was following Bessie, Ma," Sissy Three said.

"Do tell." The woman sashayed over, her dress swinging suggestively, and looked Fargo up and down as if he was a bowl of sugar and she had a sweet tooth. "I doubt Bessie is your type."

Fargo told her who he was. "I'm only interested in some water for me and my horse. Then I'll be on my way."

"What's your hurry?" She walked completely around him, smirked, and tapped a long fingernail on her chin. "My, oh, my. You're downright splendid. I'm Rose, by the way. Rose Sands. Sissy Three, here, is my youngest."

"Unusual name," Fargo remarked.

"My oldest is Sissy One; my middle girl is Sissy Two. Makes it easy to remember them that way. And it spared me a heap of arguing. My ma wanted our first to be called Mary and my husband's ma wanted her to be Sally. They were spatting something fierce. So to shut them up I went contrary to both." Rose paused. "I like your name. I like your eyes, too. They're blue like a lake."

"I think he's pretty, too, Ma," Sissy Three said.

Fargo was about to bring up the water again but just then the dirty sheet over the window moved and the twin barrels of a shotgun poked out.

"Out of the way, woman! I'm fixing to blow that pretty son of a bitch in half."

3

To Fargo's surprise, and relief, Rose Sands stepped between him and the window.

"Put that cannon down and get out here."

"Move, I say!" the man bellowed. "He has his gall, walking up here without my say so."

"I brought him, Pa," Sissy Three piped up. "He says all he wants is some water for him and his horse."

"Oh, does he, now?"

The shotgun disappeared and moments later its furious wielder filled the door from jamb to jamb if not bottom to lintel. Not much over five feet in height, the man was almost as wide as he was tall, a burly slab of brute muscle with thick eyebrows and a protruding brow. Each of his arms were as thick as both of Fargo's put together, and his hands were virtual hams with knuckles so big, they could be mistaken for walnuts. His eyes were deep set and small and shadowed by his forehead. "I'm Cletus Sands," he growled.

"Pleased to meet you," Fargo said, although he would just as soon pistol-whip the hothead. "I'd be obliged if you wouldn't point that thing at me."

Cletus had the shotgun leveled.

Rose put her hands on her shapely hips. "I told you to put that down and I meant it."

Angrily pointing the weapon at the dirt, Cletus glowered at Fargo. "I don't want you here. We don't have any water to spare. Climb on that nag of yours and skedaddle before I lose my temper."

"Pa, we have plenty of water," Sissy Three said. "It's why we're in so much trouble."

"Hush, girl," her father snapped. "We don't talk about things like that in front of strangers."

"Maybe we should," the mother remarked and, walking over to him, poked him in his broad chest. "You listen to me, Cletus, and you listen good. I won't have any of your male shenanigans, you hear me? This here gentleman is welcome to refresh himself if he wants. What's more, we're having him to supper. And you're to behave, or else."

Cletus's thick mouth twisted and Fargo thought he was going to give her a piece of his mind. Instead, Cletus meekly snarled a sarcastic, "Whatever you say, apple of my eye."

"That's better." Rose turned and bestowed as ravishing a smile as her dirty face allowed. "I trust you won't decline the invite? How about if Sissy Three takes you on around to the spring and fetches you back after you've had your drink? I need to have a few more words with my man."

"I'm grateful," Fargo said.

Right there in front of her husband, Rose grinned and winked and asked, "How much?" Then she laughed to make light of her tease. But her husband's scowl deepened.

Fargo waited until he was almost to the rear corner to ask, "Is your pa always like that?"

"Pretty much," Sissy Three answered. "I warned you he doesn't cotton to strangers. But Ma keeps him on a tight leash. She says I'll have to do the same with my husband when I'm old enough to get hitched because menfolk can't think for themselves."

A trail led into the cottonwoods. They went around a slight bend and Fargo had to firm his hold on the reins or the Ovaro would have knocked him aside to reach the inviting circle of water that lay in the shade of the tall trees.

Fargo resisted an impulse to throw himself down and

thirstily gulp. Instead, he let the stallion drink, then sank to a knee and dipped his hand in. Water never felt so wonderfully cool, or tasted so delightfully delicious as when he raised his palm to his cracked lips.

"You look like you're in heaven."

"I just about am," Fargo admitted.

Suddenly figures carrying rifles stepped out of the trees to either side, and out of habit Fargo swooped his hand to his empty holster. He felt self-conscious when he discovered they weren't Apaches but older versions of Sissy Three. Or maybe it was more fitting to say they were younger versions of Rose.

The one on the right was pushing twenty. She had tawny hair and in every other respect she was the spitting image of her mother. That included the hungry gleam that lit her eyes, and the taunting smile that curled her lips. "What have you gone and brought us, little sister? A present?"

The one on the left looked to be about sixteen. She had yet to bud into womanhood, and was too thin by half. It didn't help that unlike her sisters, she had inherited her father's bushy eyebrows and jutting brow. "He's right pretty."

Sissy Three giggled.

Fargo went on drinking. His parched throat demanded to be soothed. He paid little mind when the oldest sister came over and stood next to him, so close her hip brushed his shoulder.

"Does Ma know about this good-looking devil?" She had the same low, sultry voice as her mother.

"Who do you think had me bring him back here?" Sissy Three responded. "Pa ain't too happy, though."

"He never is when there's another rooster strutting around the coop," the oldest said. "I'm Sissy One, mister. This here is Sissy Two."

"I know," Fargo said between swallows, and pausing, he nodded at the big Sharps in the crook of her elbow. "Expecting trouble?"

Instead of answering, Sissy One turned to the youngest. "I take it he's not one of Jagger's?"

"Ma hasn't questioned him yet but I don't think he is."

Sissy Two said, "What would you know? You're too young."

"I'm as smart as you," Sissy Three bristled.

"You wish you were. Run on back to Ma, brat. Sissy One and me will watch over him."

"Ma told me to take him back, not you."

Their bickering would have gone on but the oldest stamped her bare foot and declared, "Enough! Can't you two ever get along?"

"You're a fine one to talk," Sissy Two said. "Always bossing us around like you do."

Ignoring them, Fargo cupped both hands. All he cared about was slaking his thirst. He couldn't get enough but he had to be careful; too much might bring on a stomachache. Bit by bit his overheated body cooled and he felt almost normal again. Removing his hat, he plunged it in, then upended it over his head.

Sissy Three giggled. "Look at him!"

"You're supposed to drink it, not take a bath," Sissy Two chided. "A body would think you were a fish, the way you carry on."

"Hush, you," Sissy One said. "I like a man who washes. There's not as much stink."

It was with great reluctance that Fargo stood and pulled the Ovaro away from the spring. "Too much and you'll flounder."

"Talk to your horse a lot, do you?" Sissy One teased. She ran her eyes from his face to his boots and back again. "Yes, sir. You clean up real nice. You should take off those buckskins and wash your whole body."

"Does your mother know you're a hussy?" Fargo countered, but he smiled as he said it.

"As a matter of fact, she does. But I come by it honestly. I can't help myself. I take after her."

Sissy Two snorted. "What you see in men I'll never know. They're about as worthless as teats on a boar."

"You'll think different when you're a mite older."

The youngest girl started back along the trail. "Come along, mister. We shouldn't keep Ma waiting too long."

The oldest swayed her hips suggestively. "Hope to see you again real soon, handsome."

Fargo was tempted but after what he had seen of her father, he wasn't inclined to stick around.

No sooner were they out of the cottonwoods than the heat hit them. Right away Fargo was thirsty again. It would be nice to stick around a day or two and rest up. But that brought him back to the issue of the father and that double-barreled shotgun.

"I hope you stay for supper," Sissy Three remarked over her shoulder. "We don't get many visitors these days. Not with the feud and all."

"Feud?"

Sissy Three nodded. "It's been going on a while now. So far no blood has been spilled. But Ma says it's only a matter of time."

"Who is there to feud with out here in the middle of nowhere?" Fargo asked. "I thought you had this valley all to yourselves?"

"We do," the girl confirmed. "The valley and the spring. And there's someone who doesn't like that."

Fargo remembered hearing a name. "Is it that Jagger your sister mentioned?"

"I used to like him until he turned mean. Be careful if he shows up. He's threatened to run us off, and Ma thinks he'll try one day soon. That's why we're keeping our rifles handy."

"It's not because of the Apaches?"

"Shucks, no. Oh, we watch out for them, but they've left us be ever since Ma gave them some of our blankets and one of Pa's knives." As an afterthought Sissy Three added, "Oh, and our horses."

Fargo tried to imagine why anyone would give away

their sole means of escaping that country if they had to. It was preposterous.

Rose was waiting, leaning against the wall with her hands behind her back and her body arched in an inviting bow. She could not be any more obvious if she had a sign hanging around her neck. "It's about time. I was starting to think you had drowned."

Pointedly looking at the window, Fargo asked, "Where did your husband get to?"

"He went storming off in a funk. Likely as not he'll walk halfway to New Mexico before he can control that god-awful temper of his." Rose motioned at her youngest. "Why don't you go in and set the table? Put out an extra bowl for our guest." To Fargo she said, "You will be staying for supper, won't you?" Her hooded eyes fixed on a spot below his belt. "I'm famished, myself."

"Only if your husband doesn't mind." Fargo wasn't about to be blown in half because she had an itch that needed scratching.

"Quit bringing him up. He doesn't count for anything. It's what I say that goes."

Despite his reservations, Fargo found himself admiring the smooth sweep of her long legs. "You wear the britches in your family—is that it?"

Rose languidly moved a thigh back and forth while hiking the already high hem of her dress another inch higher. "You must need spectacles. Does it look like I wear pants to you?"

Fargo chuckled. "If those are pants, they're the best pair I've set eyes on in a coon's age."

Smiling, Rose leaned toward him. "Aren't you the sweet talker? Later tonight maybe I'll give you the chance to do more than talk. That is, if you're up for a midnight stroll."

"What about your—" Fargo began.

Rose pressed a fingers to his lips. "There you go again. If I'm willing, why bring him into it? Besides, any carrying on I do is his fault."

"Is that what you tell yourself?"

Giving him a sharp look, Rose lowered her dress. "I don't much care for your airs. There's more to what you see than what you see."

"Are we talking about your legs again or something else?" Fargo asked. And it wasn't that he was putting on airs, as she called it; he didn't know where her husband, and that shotgun, had gotten to. He made up his mind to eat, ask to fill his canteen, and be on his way.

Rose grew somber. "I wish it was only my legs. I can only do so much."

"How do you mean?"

"Oh, nothing." Abruptly stiffening, Rose said out of the corner of her luscious mouth, "Here he comes. Have a care. I can control him to a point but only to a point."

Hooking his thumbs in his gun belt, and sorely wishing he had the Colt, Fargo slowly turned. "I was just thanking your wife for your hospitality."

Thunder and lightning crackled in Cletus Sands's expression. "Is that what you were doing?"

Rose said, "Don't start. I've invited him to supper and I expect you to be civil."

"Why the hell should I?"

"Because I said so," Rose shot back. "We haven't had any news of the outside world in weeks."

"Is that what you're hankering after? *News?* I suppose I'll believe that when Bessie sprouts wings and flies."

Fargo made bold to interject, "I'd just as soon be on my way. Give me my six-shooter and some water and you'll be shed of me."

"The sun can fry you to death for all I care," Cletus snapped.

"Damn your cussed hide," Rose said. "It won't hurt you to be nice for once."

"Like it hasn't hurt me all the other times?"

Fargo had put up with all he was going to. Sissy Three had gone inside with his Colt and he was set to go in after it when Rose Sands stiffened again and extended her arm.

"It appears we're about to have more visitors."

"Who the hell now?" Cletus said.

Fargo thought it would be the Jagger they had talked about. But it wasn't.

Approaching at a trot, their rifles glinting in the bright sunlight, were three Apaches.

4

The Mescaleros were widely feared, with good reason. Few tribes had killed as many whites. Not that the Mescaleros hated the white men trying to wrest their land from them more than they hated the Mexicans who had tried the same thing or the Spaniards before the Mexicans. All invaders were ripe prey.

In recent years the mere mention of their name was enough to send families racing to their root cellars or to the nearest town. Stories of Mescalero atrocities were told nightly around campfires and hearths. Stories, Fargo had learned, that often had little or no basis in fact. Rumor fed rumor until there were Mescaleros hiding behind every bush. Until the Mescaleros became more than human, they were red demons.

Even so, they were every white's worst nightmare. If taken alive, captives knew what to expect: torture and death, for most. Women were sometimes spared and made unwilling blanket mates. Children were sometimes spared, too, and raised as their own.

Few whites dared venture through Apache territory alone, as Fargo often did. Few settled far from towns and forts, as the Sands family had done. Not if they wanted to go on breathing.

Fargo's reaction on spying the three Mescaleros was typical. His gut balled into a knot and his hand once again swooped to his holster. He silently swore when his fingers closed on empty air. He took it for granted that

Cletus and Rose would dash inside but they stayed where they were. Cletus didn't even raise his shotgun.

Rose smiled warmly as if the three newcomers were the dearest of friends. To Fargo she said, "Stay still and stay quiet and we'll all live to see the sun go down."

Cletus didn't share her optimism. "I hate it when they come. We never know what they'll want next."

"Don't you dare show you're afraid of them," Rose cautioned. "They respect courage more than anything."

It had been Fargo's experience that Apaches respected resourcefulness most, whether in their own kind or in an enemy. A clever foe was held in higher regard than a brave one.

"Sissy One and Sissy Two are back by the spring," Cletus said.

"Keep calm. The girls have their rifles and are good shots. If these three want water, we'll go with them."

"I hate it," Cletus said again.

Rose moved past him, smoothed her dress and waited. Outwardly she was calm but Fargo suspected that her insides were churning.

The three warriors slowed to a walk when they were about fifty feet out. The one in the middle was slightly ahead of the other two. A headband encircled his raven hair. Swarthy and square-jawed, he wore a long-sleeved shirt and leggings despite the heat. A bandoleer crossed his chest, and in a sheath on his left hip was a long-handled knife.

"That one is Three Ears," Rose said. "Could be you've heard of him."

Indeed Fargo had. Everyone knew about Three Ears. Years ago, when still a youth, the warrior took part in a raid south of the border. The raiders stole many horses and slew many Mexicans. But at one point, a farmer armed with a machete slashed at him. The young Apache managed to twist his head so that instead of having his skull cleaved, the machete cut his ear in half.

The ear never knit, and the two halves lent the illusion he had two small ears on that side. Ever since, he had been known as Three Ears. His hatred of Mexicans was legendary. It was said he had made it his life's work to slay as many as he could before he went into the ground.

Now the three drew rein some ten feet out. Three Ears immediately focused on Fargo.

"A pleasure to see you again," Rose greeted him. "Our friends are always welcome."

Three Ears grunted.

"Our house is your house; our food is your food; our water is your water," Rose went on. "Climb down and stay a spell."

"Yes," Cletus echoed, but his tone belied his true feelings.

Three Ears had not taken his dark eyes off Fargo. "Who this white-eye?" he demanded.

"Another friend of ours," Rose said.

Fargo noticed that the Mescalero glanced at his empty holster. He felt defenseless, and hated it. If the three attacked, he would be hard pressed to preserve his life.

"We find his tracks. We follow," Three Ears said.

A chill ran down Fargo's spine. They must have found the body of the warrior he had slain, and they were here for revenge. He edged toward the Ovaro, and the Henry in the saddle scabbard.

"Our friend and his people do not miss much," Rose said.

"My people see all, know all," Three Ears boasted. "We know Big Beard want water. We know him try take. We know there be fight."

Cletus gave a slight start. "You'll help us, then? As our friend and all?"

Three Ears did not hide his contempt. "No."

"Why not? After all we've given you?"

"You give so you stay Apache land. You not give so Apache fight enemies," was Three Ear's reply.

"But our enemies are your enemies," Cletus persisted despite a warning look from his wife. "Besides, what has Big Beard ever done for you?"

A sly smile curled Three Ears's mouth. He patted his rifle. "What you think he do?"

"He gave guns to your people? That's against the law."

"White law for whites," Three Ears said.

Cletus wouldn't give up. "But he has six men riding for him. All I have are my girls and my woman."

Three Ears motioned toward Rose. "Your woman smart. You put up good fight."

"And maybe die. But with your help we can beat Jagger. With your help my family will be safe."

"All things die. People die. Animals die. You afraid maybe you die, Always Angry?"

Fargo had to hand it to the Apaches. The names they picked for themselves and for their enemies always fit. In Cletus's case, they had spied on the Sandses enough to realize his temper always got the best of him.

"I'm not scared of anything," Cletus blustered. "I just don't want my family killed, is all. You wouldn't want yours killed, either, damn you."

"Hush, now," Rose said to him.

But Three Ears had not taken offense. "Our women fight. My wives fight. They strong like men."

"You have more than one wife?" Rose asked.

Three Ears held up three fingers, then indulged in a rare smile. "One wife Mexican. Beat her every day."

"Dear Lord," Rose said.

"I would never hit a woman," Cletus said.

"You lie, white-eye. We see you hit your girls with sticks. Maybe one time you hit them, they shoot you."

One of the other Mescaleros grinned, showing that he, too, spoke some English.

By then Fargo was close enough to the Ovaro, and the saddle scabbard, to reach his rifle in a single bound if he had to.

"Can I interest you in some food?" Rose asked the Apaches. "Or is it water you came for?"

"We came—" Three Ears said, and then stopped. Without any explanation, he wheeled his mount and jabbed his heels and the trio departed at a trot, raising dust in their wake.

"What in hell was that all about?" Cletus marveled, more to himself than to them. "Why did they leave like that?"

"I don't know," Rose admitted. "But I don't like it. Not one little bit. We have enough trouble without the Apaches acting up."

Fargo was glad to see them go. But now he had a new concern. If he was right, and Three Ears wanted revenge, then the three might wait out there for him to ride off and jump him when he least expected. Apaches never attacked unless they had an edge. Kill without being killed was their byword.

Cletus ran a dirty hand through his dirty hair. "I hate this place more every day. And thanks to you, we're stuck here."

"I'll thank you not to take that tone with me," Rose said angrily. "I've done what I had to so we can survive."

"I know better," Cletus said. He bestowed another scowl on Fargo, then turned and tramped around the side of the cabin.

Rose sighed, her shoulders slumping. "I try. Honest to God I do. But that man would try the patience of a saint."

"Why do you put up with it?"

"Why else?" was Rose's rejoinder. "I love the infernal lunkhead. He claimed my heart when I was sixteen and I still love him despite his flaws. His drinking, his temper, the violence. I put up with it for years. And I'll be honest with you." She smiled. "Planting root here was the smartest thing I ever did."

It struck Fargo as about the stupidest notion ever, but he held his tongue except to say, "Is that a fact?"

"Cletus hasn't had a drop of liquor in two years. Better yet, he's not behind bars where that wretched judge wanted to throw him."

"From what your daughter told me, he brought it on himself," Fargo commented.

"Sissy Three? She's young. She doesn't see the world as it truly is. Take her words for what they are worth but she lacks a few of the facts." Rose straightened. "Now then. How about that meal I promised? Give me half an hour and it will be ready."

Fargo was left alone. He had neglected to ask for his revolver back but he would remedy that soon enough. Since it might be a while before he left, he decided to strip the Ovaro and give the stallion extra relief from the stifling heat. It might also trick the Apaches into thinking he intended to stay the night.

"Ma says I'm to keep you company."

Sissy Three was back.

Fargo went on undoing the cinch. "Where did you get to?"

"I was watching the redskins out the window. If they'd so much as lifted a finger against Ma or Pa, I'd have blown them to kingdom come."

"Killed a lot of them, have you?"

"Not yet. But I could if I had to."

"And you're how old?"

Sissy Three resented the question. "Old enough to squeeze the trigger. I've shot rabbits and deer. Shooting people won't be any different."

"That's where you're wrong." Fargo had put lead into more than his share. It took a special sort of courage.

"I'll prove it to you if they come back."

"I hope you never have to. Killing leaves a scar. Not outside where people can see but inside where only you feel it."

"Even if it has to be done?"

"Even if," Fargo confirmed. Sometimes, at night, he would wake up covered with sweat and filled with regret.

"The Apaches have killed a lot of folks and they get by," Sissy Three noted.

"Apaches train themselves to forget."

"If they can, I can."

"You're a little young to be a heartless killer," Fargo told her.

"My sister shot a man once and I'm no different than her."

"I thought we were done talking about that." But Fargo was curious. "Which sister? And who did she shoot?"

"It was Sissy One."

Fargo couldn't get used to their names. How much effort did it take to give babies new names and not number them like they were cattle?

The girl lowered her voice. "She shot Butch Jagger."

"Is he any relation to Earl Jagger?"

"Butch is Earl's son. He cottoned to Sissy One and asked her to be his wife but she doesn't want anything to do with him. When he got mad and tried to drag her off, she shot him in the foot."

"Not in the heart or the head?"

"She didn't want Butch dead. She just wanted him to quit pestering her. She told me she aimed at the center of his foot but he moved it just as she fired and she blew off his toe by accident."

"I take it he was mad?"

"Mostly he bawled like a baby and blubbered for his pa. So our pa took him home, and that's when the Jaggers and us had what Ma calls a falling out."

"Shooting off toes will do that."

"Now they're even madder because of the water. They hardly have any and they want to use our spring but Ma and Pa told them they can't."

"Does your family ever do anything the easy way?"

"Pardon me?"

"Never mind," Fargo said.

"We're sure in a fix."

"I'd say so. You're stranded with no way to leave because you tore your wagon up to make your cabin and you gave your horses to the Mescaleros so you could live on their land. But they could turn on you at any time. And now you have this Earl Jagger mad at you over his son being shot and threatening to take your water. Does that about sum things up?"

"Pretty much." Unexpectedly, Sissy Three clasped his hand. "We need help, mister. We need help bad." She squeezed his fingers. "Please. For me. I'm too young to die."

"Oh, hell," Skye Fargo said.

5

It came time for supper and Rose called the oldest girls in from the spring. Cletus objected, saying as how one should stand guard in case the Jaggers paid them a visit. Rose silenced him with a wifely look and the remark, "We're a family and we'll eat as a family and that's that."

Their cabin had a dirt floor. Their furniture consisted of an old oak table so battered and banged up, it wobbled when Fargo bumped it with his leg as he was sitting down. They had four chairs in the same condition. Over against the rear wall was a settee. One of its legs was missing so they had propped it up with an overturned bucket.

"Our home sweet home," Rose said as she ladled stew into the chipped bowl she had placed in front of him.

The aroma gave Fargo a clue to the contents. "Squirrel?"

"How did you guess? Yes, you're in for a treat. We don't have it often as there aren't a lot of the little critters to be had. You must have been born under a lucky star."

Fargo picked up the large wooden spoon they had given him, and stirred. In addition to chunks of squirrel, some of which had a few tufts of hair attached, she had added small bits of potato and a few small carrots and just enough flour to give the stew the consistency of water.

"I love squirrel stew," Sissy Three said eagerly, about

to dig in. "The only thing I like more is when we have cricket soup."

Fargo wasn't sure he had heard right. "Cricket soup?"

"I like how they crunch when you bite them. And if you bite the right part, they're as juicy as an apple. I always forget to peel the legs and they prick at my throat as they go down."

Fargo was fast losing his appetite. It sounded to him as if they were barely eking out a living. "There must be deer hereabouts. How about if I go hunting for you?"

Cletus was his usual surly self. "I go hunting all the time. But it's not as easy as it was back in Georgia. There's not as much game and the animals are a lot more skittish."

"I'll try anyway," Fargo offered.

Cletus opened his mouth, evidently to object.

"You do that," Rose interjected. "We'd be ever so grateful."

The older girls were being strangely quiet. Sissy Two kept glancing at Sissy One and then at Fargo. He couldn't figure out why and figured she would tell him if and when she wanted. Dipping his spoon into his bowl, he tried a taste. As stews went, it was just this side of bath water.

And as if she could read his mind, Rose said, "It lacks salt and seasoning, I know. But I'm plumb out."

Fargo decided to bite the bullet. "You can't go on living like this." They had been lucky so far, damned lucky, but no one's luck held forever.

"It's the drought. We ate better before the heat hit. When we first came here, there was plenty of game."

But by now, Fargo reflected, they had killed most of the game off, and drought or no drought, they would be at starvation's door before too long. Without horses, they were doomed, yet they didn't seem to realize it.

"We try to grow things," Rose had gone on. "I had some seeds in the wagon. Carrots. Potatoes. Corn. Peas.

But nothing does well here. The soil is as poor as any I've ever come across."

"Back to Georgia we had a wonderful vegetable patch." Sissy One broke her silence.

"We never went hungry," Sissy Two said.

Cletus said gruffly, "Enough of that kind of talk. We make do the best we can."

"I was only saying, Pa," Sissy One told him.

"And you," Cletus said, jabbing a thick finger at Fargo. "Who are you to sit here at our table and tell us what we can and can't do?"

"This was my idea," Rose brought up again, but whether she was referring to having Fargo to supper, or to living in that remote valley, she didn't make clear.

Fargo chewed on a piece of squirrel. Suddenly his tongue stung, as if from a bee sting. Reaching into his mouth, he pulled out a splinter of bone.

"Sorry." Rose smiled. "I should have warned you. I might have missed a few when I was chopping the varmint up."

Fargo needed a drink, and he wasn't the only one.

Licking his lips, Cletus wrung his hands and said, "Do you know what I miss most?"

"Don't start," Rose said.

"I can't help it. It's been two years. There are days when it doesn't bother me, and there are bad days like today." Cletus glanced at Fargo. "I don't suppose you have a flask in your saddlebags? Or better yet, a bottle? Anything will do. Whiskey. Rum. Hell, I'd even drink cough syrup if you had some."

Fargo shook his head. "I never drink on the trail."

"It figures. Once again the Almighty laughs in my face," Cletus said sorrowfully.

"Cut it out," Rose said. "You whine like a baby. I would have thought you had the craving out of your system by now."

"Thank Earl Jagger for that."

Rose colored, leaving Fargo to wonder what Cletus meant.

"Let's just eat, shall we? Without all this bickering? We have company, for goodness' sake."

"Good-looking company," Sissy One commented.

"Behave yourself, daughter," Rose said. "We're at table and you'll act like a lady."

"She can't help herself," Cletus came to his oldest daughter's defense. "It runs in her blood."

Thankfully, everyone fell quiet. Fargo ate but his heart wasn't in it. Or his stomach. He would as soon eat the pemmican he had in his saddlebags but he didn't have enough for all of them so he didn't mention it.

The Sandses had two helpings except for Sissy Three, who had three, and the habit of loudly smacking her lips after each mouthful.

Fargo waited until they were about done to fish for more information. "What can you tell me about the Jagger spread?"

Cletus was instantly suspicious. "Why do you want to know?"

"Hush," Rose scolded. "They call it the Bar J. It's a rawhide outfit. I'm surprised they've stuck here as long as they have."

"There are reasons and there are reasons," Cletus said sourly.

Ignoring him, Rose continued. "They had a spring like we do but their spring has about gone dry. I expect they'll pack up and move on. Earl Jagger has made noise about using our spring but we refused to let him. Their cows would drink us dry in no time."

"He has six men riding for him?" Fargo recalled.

"Plus his boy. Butch, his name is. He used to come courting Sissy One but they had a falling out."

"Shooting off a man's toe will do that."

"Oh, you've heard, then?" Rose laughed. "Yes, that was a pity. But he has nine toes left. He shouldn't ought to have made such a fuss over it."

Fargo pushed back his chair. "If you'll excuse me, I'd like to let my horse drink again before I turn in."

Cletus instantly growled, "You're staying the night?"

"Why shouldn't he?" Rose asked. "The sun will set soon, and him and his pinto are tuckered out. I'm happy to have them."

"You would be."

"One thing," Fargo said, holding out his right hand. "I want my Colt."

"No."

"I think we should give it to him," Rose said.

"I said no and I meant no."

"I've proven I'm not out to harm you." Fargo glanced about the room. "Where is it?"

"No," Cletus said again.

Rose was growing mad. "I'll tell you what. Why don't you go water your horse while my husband and me have a little talk?"

"Flap your gums all you want, woman, but you won't change my mind," Cletus said.

Both had apparently forgotten that Fargo's rifle was still in his saddle scabbard. "I'll go," he said. "But when I get back, I'm taking it." He stared straight at Cletus. "Whether you like it or not."

Twilight painted the valley in shades of gray. A welcome if only slightly cool breeze fanned Fargo's face as he led the stallion around to the trail into the cottonwoods. He was thinking of the Sandses, and he shouldn't have been. He should have stayed alert. For no sooner did he step around the bend than a Remington revolver was shoved in his face. At the click of the hammer, Fargo imitated the trees.

"Not a peep out of you," warned the man holding the six-gun, "or I'll splatter your brains." He was young, with a round face and no chin to speak of, and watery eyes that gave the impression he was about to burst into tears. He moved to one side, limping. The tip of his boot had a hole in it.

"You must be Butch Jagger."
"How do you know that?"
"I heard about your toe."
Butch grew red in the face. He pointed the Remington at Fargo's cheek. "Who are you, anyhow?"
"A friend of the Sands's," Fargo stretched the truth considerably. He was tempted to teach the youngster not to wave six-shooters in someone's face, but just then two more men materialized, both with their revolvers out.
"Where is she?" Butch asked.
"Who?"
"Don't treat me like I'm stupid. Who else would I mean but that damn vixen who shot me?"
"Maybe you should quit while you're nine toes ahead," Fargo advised.
Butch Jagger blinked. The tallest of his companions laughed, which made Jagger's round face grow darker. "You think you're funny, don't you, stranger? How about if I pistol-whip you? Swallowing a few broken teeth should cure you of that."
"We've got no quarrel with him," said the tall man. His clothes, hat and boots marked him as a cowhand. Their condition marked him as a cowhand in need of better pay.
"Did I ask you, Vern?" Butch snapped. Gripping the front of Fargo's shirt, Butch shook him. But he wasn't strong enough to do more than make Fargo sway. "I won't ask a third time. Where is the love of my life?"
"You still care for her after she shot your toe off?"
"Why wouldn't I? She and me are meant for each other even if she doesn't agree."
"So this is how it is," Fargo said, and sighed. "If it's not chickens, it's feathers."
"What?"
"Nothing. Listen, boy. I'm not your enemy. I'm only passing through. I'd have been gone by now but they took my Colt."

Butch glanced at Fargo's empty holster. Suddenly he stiffened. "Did you just call me *boy*?"

"Uh-oh," Vern said.

The third cowboy, older by a score of years and scruffier by half, chuckled and said, "You shouldn't ought to have done that, mister. If there's one thing that boy hates, it's being called a boy."

Butch glared at him. "Damn you, Fowler. I'll take abuse from my pa but I'll be damned if I'll take it from anyone else."

Fargo had their measure and didn't feel as if he was in any great danger. The love-struck toeless Romeo was more bluster than anything else, and the cowhands were not out to hurt anyone.

"Where is she, damn it?"

"The last I saw Sissy One, she was chewing on squirrel fat."

"Damn my luck," Butch said, gazing down the trail. "But she's bound to come out sooner or later. We'll wait. And you'll do exactly as I say or I'll put windows in your skull."

"He's a regular badman," Vern said.

"He must have shot fifty men or better," Fowler threw in, and snickered. "A man-killer if ever there was one."

"I get no respect, I tell you," Butch complained. "Not even from my pa's own hands. I bet if I shot you they'd respect me."

Fowler snorted. "What's to respect about shooting an unarmed man?"

Fargo brushed past Butch and led the Ovaro over to the spring. He hoped that was the end of it but he should have known better.

"You can't just walk off when a man is holding a gun on you. Don't you have a lick of sense?"

"I'm beginning to wonder."

"Who are you, anyhow?"

Instead of answering, Fargo asked, "Is it true your

ranch has about gone dry and you plan to help yourselves to the Sands's water?"

"They've told you everything, haven't they? But you can't blame us for asking them to share. We'll lose all our cows if they don't."

"It's their spring."

"My pa says that doesn't give them the right to ruin us. When he gets here he'll—"

"Hush, you consarned infant," Fowler said.

The next second Fargo heard the *twang* of a bow string and then the *thwack* of a feathered shaft imbedding itself in the older cowboy's ribs.

"Injuns!" Butch screeched.

Fargo dived for the ground as a war whoop pierced the air.

6

Fowler staggered back in shock. Then the pain hit him and he let out a loud cry, part roar of rage and part bellow of agony. He clawed for his six-shooter, but already the arrow had done its deadly deed and his life was fast fading.

Butch Jagger, down on one knee, banged off several wild shots while shouting, "Where are they? Where are they?"

Vern had drawn his revolver but he didn't waste lead. Scuttling over to Fowler, he looped an arm around the older cowboy's drooping shoulders. "How bad is it?"

Fowler's lips moved but all that came out was scarlet. He gurgled a few times, his legs went rigid, and he was gone.

Fargo hugged the earth. He expected more arrows but after half a minute had gone by without any, he leaped up, darted to the Ovaro, and yanked the Henry from the scabbard. Levering a round into the chamber, he probed the cottonwoods. The sun was almost gone and gloom shrouded the pale boles. Not so much as a fly stirred.

"We have to get out of here," Vern said to Butch.

"And leave Fowler's body? We can't do that. He's ridden for my pa for years. It wouldn't be right."

"The Sands," Vern said. "They'll have heard the shots, and that loco bastard will come running."

Fargo didn't need to ask who he meant.

"Cletus did threaten to kill me," Butch nervously remarked. "I suppose we better fan the breeze."

Vern was easing Fowler to the ground. "Whatever we're going to do, we'd better do it quick. The Apaches might find our horses if they haven't already."

"Our horses!" Butch exclaimed, and, breaking into a mad sprint, he dashed off.

"Damn fool kid," Vern said, and ran after him.

Snatching hold of the Ovaro's dangling reins, Fargo backed toward the trail. From the cabin came yells. He stopped at the bend to await them, his gaze falling on Fowler. Why only the one arrow? he asked himself. Ordinarily, Apaches pressed their attack until their enemies were dead or routed. He suspected there had been just one warrior and now that warrior was gone.

"What's going on?"

"What was all the shooting about?"

The Sandses rushed up, everyone with a rifle except for Cletus, who had his shotgun. He shoved past Fargo and saw Fowler. "It's one of Jagger's men! With an arrow in him!" Turning every which way, Cletus waved the shotgun. "What the hell is this? Where did the red devils get to?"

Rose was her usual calm self. She stopped next to Fargo and coolly regarded the body. "Fill us in."

Fargo went to reply but her husband suddenly sprang toward them and thrust the shotgun at him.

"What the hell are you doing with that rifle? Hand it over right this second."

Fargo saw that in Cletus's excitement, he had forgotten to thumb back the twin hammers. And unfortunately for Cletus, Fargo had put up with all he was going to. Without saying a word, and with no warning whatsoever, he drove the Henry's stock into Cletus's gut with enough force to double Cletus over. Cletus sputtered and cursed and fumbled at the shotgun. "Some jackasses never learn," Fargo said, and slammed the stock against the idiot's head.

Cletus Sands folded like a house of cards and lay senseless at his feet.

Rose and her girls were rooted in surprise.

"Where's my Colt?" Fargo demanded.

"We left it inside," Rose said, her eyes on her husband's motionless form. "You didn't bust his skull, did you?"

"You don't see what few brains he has leaking out, do you?" Fargo rejoined. To Sissy Two, who was standing nearest, he said, "Fetch my revolver. And keep your eyes peeled for Apaches."

The middle girl glanced at Rose. "Should I, Ma?"

Fargo towered over her. "You'll get it, and you'll get it now." His tone impelled her into whirling and racing away.

"You shouldn't talk to my girls like that," Rose said.

Fargo went to the body. Fowler's eyes were open, and he closed them. He gave the arrow a tug but it was lodged fast. It would have to be cut out.

"I'd sure like to hear what happened," Rose said.

Briefly, Fargo told them. At his mention of Butch Jagger, Sissy One gave a start and became the same color as a beet.

Rose, though, chuckled. "So he still wants my girl after she shot off his toe? That's what I call true love."

Fargo called it stupid but he didn't say so out loud. He mentioned his belief there was only one Apache. "He could have put an arrow into any of us but it was Fowler's day to die." Although, now that he thought about it, the warrior might have loosed the shaft at Butch Jagger, who had turned a split second before Fowler was hit.

"Three Ears gave me his word his people would leave us be," Rose said. "I trusted him."

Fargo was surprised. Most whites wouldn't trust a red man as far as they could throw a buffalo. "It wasn't one of your family."

"That's right," Rose said, and appeared profoundly relieved. "Maybe everything is all right after all."

Cletus groaned.

"Splash water on his face and let's get everyone inside," Fargo suggested. "I'll bring the cowboy." Squatting, he set down the Henry, slid his hands under Fowler's arms, and lifted. It took some doing but he hoisted the body over his shoulder, reclaimed his rifle, and stood. He was halfway to the cabin when Sissy Three dashed up, half out of breath, and held out his Colt. "My hands are full. Stick it in my holster."

"My pa is going to be awful mad at you."

"He brought it on himself."

Her expression became troubled. "He's not very nice at times, I'm sorry to say."

"I've met grizzlies who were nicer."

Sissy Three grinned but the grin was fleeting. "It used to be worse back when he was drinking. He'd yell at Ma and us and once he hit her but she walloped him with her frying pan and he hasn't hit her since." She hesitated. "Do you ever act like he does?"

"I've been drunk a few times," Fargo admitted.

"No, I mean do you ever hit women? Ma says some men do it all the time. I'd hate to marry a man like that."

They were rounding the rear of the cabin, and Fargo slowed. He sensed that this was important to her, and remembering how she had clasped his hand, he answered, "Not all men are like your pa."

"You're not, are you?"

"I've never hit a woman unless she was trying to stick a knife in me or fill me with lead."

"That's good to hear. I think when I grow up, I'd like to marry a man like you. You're nice, and you're pretty."

"There you go again," Fargo said.

"What? Oh. Sorry. You're nice and you're handsome." Sissy Three giggled.

Fargo placed the body down under the front window. As he turned, Cletus came barreling around the corner.

"You hit me, you—"

"Not another word," Fargo said, his hand on his Colt.

Cletus bared his teeth and started to raise the shotgun, but stopped. Uncertainty crossed his face, and a trace of something else. He gave a slight cough, pivoted, and went inside.

"He's scared of you," Sissy Three said.

"You better go in, too," Fargo advised. "I need to dig out the arrow." He would spare her the sight.

"I've never seen anybody do that. Can I watch?"

"No."

Frowning, Sissy Three reluctantly obeyed. No sooner did she disappear than out came her mother.

"We need to talk."

Fargo hunkered, hiked his pant leg, and slid his fingers into his boot. The hilt of the Arkansas toothpick molded to his hand.

"Didn't you hear me? I have a request to make of you. It's asking a lot, I know, since we hardly know each other. But you're the only one who can help."

"Help in what?" Fargo asked as he bent and applied the razor tip to the dead man's shirt.

"I want you to take me and my family out of here."

Fargo would not have been more dumbfounded if she sprouted horns and a tail.

"Hear me out. So long as the Apaches left us be, I was content to stay. It was best for my family, especially for Cletus. So long as he can't get his hands on booze, he's fine. But alcohol poisons him. It turns him into a mad beast. These past two years he was able to dry out and now he's a whole new man."

Given what Fargo had seen of Cletus Sands, sobriety wasn't much of an improvement. Then insight dawned. "Is that the reason you stayed here all this time?"

"It sure is. You can't imagine what it was like before. There wasn't a night he didn't come home drunk, half the time bruised and bloody from fighting." Rose gazed out across the valley. "This might not seem like much to you, but it's the best we've ever had it. The peace. The quiet. Having him sober."

Fargo regarded her in a whole new light.

"He's treated our girls better, too. Used to be, he was forever carping about their chores and punishing them for this or that. But not anymore."

Recalling that Cletus had practically begged him for a drink, Fargo said, "He still feels the need."

"I know. It's a risk I'll take. We can't stay, not with the Apaches and Earl Jagger both out to do us harm."

Fargo wondered if she realized what she was asking. He had the only horse. With them on foot, it would take weeks to reach the nearest outpost. Weeks of burning sun and the ever-present threat of hostiles.

"It will take a couple of days for Earl Jagger to get here. We can be long gone by then."

"I'll think about it," Fargo said.

"What's to think about? You and my youngest have been right friendly. Do you want her to end up like this cowboy?"

"No one would hurt a girl her age."

"You don't know that. And I'd rather she was safe than take the chance of losing her." Rose placed a hand on his shoulder. "What do you say? Will you help? We can be ready to leave at sunrise."

Fargo didn't say anything.

"Please. I'm a mother with three girls and we're in a predicament only you can get us out of."

"There's your husband."

Rose snorted. "You saw him today. Even though he hasn't had a lick of liquor in a coon's age, he still has that temper of his. And he's not a scout, like you. He's never fought Injuns."

"I'll think about it," Fargo said again.

And think he did, until well past midnight. A parson would say the right thing to do was lend them a hand. But they had brought this on themselves. Or at least the mother and father had. The girls hadn't done anything except have simpletons for parents.

A hand behind his head, Fargo gazed up at the sparkling stars that filled the firmament and wondered how in hell he had gotten himself into this mess. As much as he wanted to ride on, he couldn't. Rose had discerned his weakness. Sissy Three was young and sweet and innocent, and she didn't deserve to be made an orphan or the unwilling wife of an Apache. He tried to tell himself that these people were nothing to him, that he didn't owe them a thing. But then he would remember Sissy Three taking his hand, and saying how she didn't want to die, and he would curse the soft heart he didn't realize he had.

It was pushing one in the morning when Fargo rolled onto his side and closed his eyes. If he had any sense at all, he would quietly saddle up and get the blazes out of there. But so long as he had a shred of—of what? Goodness? Conscience?—he was stuck.

Finally, Fargo slept. And dreamed. And in one of his dreams, he was in a field covered by mist and a pair of eyes was staring at him. Eerie eyes, a lot like a mountain lion's, only these were red and filled with hate so potent, he could feel it in his bones. And then the mist parted, and the red eyes belonged to Three Ears, and Three Ears was scalping Sissy Three.

Fargo woke up. He was covered with sweat, and uneasy. "Hell," he said. Annoyed at himself, he closed his eyes but it was a while before slumber again claimed him.

As was his habit, Fargo was up at the crack of dawn. He was hungry, but he had something to do first. It was dark inside the cabin and he couldn't see the Sandses, who were sleeping at the back of the room. He quietly snuck out and went over to the body.

Planting Fowler would take some doing without a shovel or a pick. The ground was as hard as iron.

Fargo was standing there mulling what to do when an ominous rumble warned him of an impending storm. Not the kind that came with roiling black clouds and the crack of lightning. This storm was man-made, and came in the form of seven riders who were galloping up the valley toward the cabin. The rider out in front had a bushy black beard.

His Henry in hand, Fargo moved to meet them, saying out loud, "This is a hell of a way to start the day."

7

So much for Rose claiming it would take Earl Jagger two to three days to show up. Earl was easy to spot—he had the bushiest beard Fargo ever saw, and that took some doing. Butch Jagger and the cowhand called Vern were with him.

The elder Jagger brought his roan to a stop and sat regarding Fargo as he might a snake he had just found under a rock.

"Who the hell are you?"

"Morning," Fargo said.

"I asked you a question."

"I didn't answer."

Earl Jagger had a craggy face that brought to mind granite, and cold eyes that brought to mind icy mountain heights. "In case no one has told you, I don't abide jackasses."

"That makes two of us," Fargo told him.

A skinny puncher who evidently fancied himself a shootist and wore two Smith and Wessons kneed his sorrel closer. "Let me teach this hombre some manners, Mr. Jagger."

"Sheathe your claws, Reese," Earl Jagger said. "I swat my own flies." He placed his big hands on his saddle horns and leaned forward, those cold eyes of his shifting to the pale form of Fowler. "They tell me it was Apaches."

Fargo had left the arrow lying next to the dead man. Picking it up, he handed it to the rancher. "See for yourself. I cut it out and was fixing to bury him."

Earl Jagger studied the shaft. "This is Apache, sure enough. Those damn Mescaleros. I'd as soon they were all six feet under." In a fit of anger he snapped the arrow in half and threw the two pieces away. "It's true what they say. The only good Injun is a dead Injun."

"Depends on your point of view."

"Injun lover, are you? It's too bad there's so many dumb people in this world."

"Take your men and go," Fargo said.

Earl Jagger's fingers opened and closed as if they were around a throat. "No one tells me what to do, mister. Ever."

Fargo took a step to the left so he had a better view of Reese. The two-gun man would be the first to draw if it came to lead and gun smoke. "For a rawhide outfit, you sure do put on airs."

"And for one hombre against seven, you sure don't know when to keep your mouth shut."

"Start the dance," Fargo said.

Reese poised his arms, ready to jerk his pistols. "Did you hear him, Mr. Jagger? Say the word."

"My ears work just fine, Reese," the rancher said flatly. "And I won't tell you again about those claws of yours." He stared at the closed cabin door. "Where are the Sands? It's time this came to a head."

"You're talking about their water?"

"My own stream has gone dry and my cattle will die if I don't find more."

"Why here?"

Earl Jagger gestured sharply. "Because everywhere else is bone-dry, too. It's the worst drought I've ever seen." He gestured again, this time at the tops of the cottonwoods visible behind the cabin. "That spring of theirs is the only water left for a hundred miles around. It can save my cows."

"I told your son. I'll tell you. It's their spring."

"I'm willing to pay for the privilege. I want to be fair. But they refuse. That bitch Rose said I could go jump off a cliff. That it would be a cold day in hell before she'd let me or mine take a sip from her precious spring."

Fargo could imagine Rose saying that. "It's not up to me."

"If it were, you'd let me? I appreciate that. But where exactly do you stand in this? What's your interest? If I push will you shove back?"

Reese had not lowered his hands. "I'd like to see him try."

"Shut the hell up," Earl Jagger commanded.

Fargo was wondering why Cletus and Rose hadn't come out. They had to have heard the rancher ride up, and all the talk right outside their door. "Why don't you come back another time?" By then he and the Sandses would be gone.

"What the hell for? I'm here now." Earl Jagger raised his voice. "Rose? I know you can hear me in there. We need to have words, woman."

Fargo was struck by the fact the rancher had called out to the wife and not the husband. The door, though, didn't open, and there were no sounds from within.

"What the hell?" Earl Jagger said.

"I guess they don't want to talk to you."

"They will whether they want to or not." Earl swung down, his saddle creaking under his weight. "I was on my way over here when I ran into my son on his way back to the ranch." Earl glanced in disgust at his offspring. "He came over to see that damn girl again."

"Sissy One," Fargo said.

"That's the tart. She's not a whore but she's as close as a female gets without asking for money." Earl Jagger moved toward the door but Fargo stepped in front of him.

"Out of the way."

"No."

"Don't be dumb. You can't stop me. Ask them to come out and we'll hash this over."

"If they wanted to talk, they'd be out here by now." Fargo was keeping an eye on the hands. All it would take was the right spark. "I'm asking you again to go."

"You want me to ride all the way home and then come all the way back? Are you loco? I'll have this out with them here and now, and neither you nor anyone else will stop me."

"I don't push easy," Fargo warned.

"I can tell," Earl Jagger said. "But I have to do it. My cattle need water right this minute, not a week from now." He jerked a thumb over his shoulder. "Or don't your eyes work?"

Fargo looked and saw what he should have seen earlier. Bunched at the mouth of the valley were hundreds of cattle. "Is that your whole herd?"

"Every last head," Earl Jagger confirmed. "When I said they need water *now*, I wasn't fooling."

Fargo sympathized. He truly did. A rancher's cows were his livelihood. The drought had Jagger teetering on the brink of ruin, and Jagger was doing what he needed to do in order to survive. Were Fargo in Jagger's boots, he would do the same. "The Sands are worried your cattle will drink their spring dry."

"Could well be," Earl admitted. "I'll be sorry if that happens, as much for me as for Rose and her family."

Fargo sensed the rancher was sincere.

"Life can be hell. I hate having to do this. But my back is to the wall." Earl Jagger turned to the window and the dirty sheet that covered it. "I know you can hear me in there, Rose. Come out so we can settle this."

The sheet moved, and the twin barrels of the shotgun were trained on the rancher.

Reese's hands flashed to his pistols. Several of the others, Butch among them, stiffened in alarm. But Earl Jagger wasn't ruffled, and said flatly, "Blow me in half and my men will burn this sorry excuse for a house to the ground, and you along with it."

There was no reply.

"Rose, is that you? Or is it that worthless husband of yours holding that twelve-gauge? Come out here so we can talk."

Fargo was puzzled by the continued silence from inside. What *were* the Sandses playing at?

"Act your age, damn it," Earl Jagger snapped. "I'm trying to be reasonable. The least you could do is meet me halfway."

Once again no one answered him.

The rancher glanced at Fargo and Fargo shrugged to show he had no idea what was going on.

"I will count to five," Earl Jagger announced. "If you haven't shown yourself by then, I'm coming in." He paused. "One."

Fargo heard whispering but he couldn't make out the words. Suddenly coming to a decision, he grabbed the barrel and wrenched. Someone bleated in surprise as the shotgun came loose. The sheet moved just enough for them to see who had been holding it.

"What in the world?" Earl Jagger said.

Fargo pushed the sheet out of the way and stared in bewilderment at Sissy Two. "What are you up to, girl? Where are your parents?"

"Gone," she said fearfully. "Please don't hurt me. I was only doing as Ma told me to when we're home alone."

"We?" Fargo said.

The door opened and out came Sissy Three. "Don't be mad. We're never to let on when Ma and Pa are gone."

Fargo was as surprised as Earl Jagger. "Where did they go?"

"To find Sissy One."

"I'm confused," Earl Jagger said. "You're not making any sense."

"Sissy One snuck out last night, like she does sometimes. Only Ma was awake and heard her, and Ma woke up Pa, and they both snuck out after her to see where she was going."

Fargo hadn't heard anything, but then he hadn't paid

much attention when one or the other of them got up to go out. He'd assumed they were heeding nature's call.

"They haven't returned yet?" Earl Jagger said. "What time was it they left, girl?"

"We don't have a clock but it wasn't long after we turned in. I'd just fallen asleep and Ma woke me to tell me what they were doing, and to stay inside with Sissy Two until they got back."

"Have your folks ever been gone this long before?" Fargo wanted to know.

Sissy Three shook her head. "Sissy Two and me are starting to get worried. Pa took his revolver but he's not much of a shot."

Earl Jagger turned to Fargo. "What do you make of this? I'd say it was a trick only I know how much Rose loves these girls. She'd never go off and leave them alone this long."

Butch Jagger had an opinion. "Something must have happened to them, Pa."

"My boy, the genius."

"Sissy One could be in trouble," Butch said anxiously. "We need to find them."

"Like hell we do," Earl said. "We're here to water our cows and nothing else. I can't spare you to go gallivanting off to search for them, so don't even ask me."

"But Sissy One probably snuck out to see me," Butch argued. "She must have thought I was still close by."

"Oh, it wasn't you she went to meet," Sissy Three informed him.

Shocked but trying not to show it, Butch said, "If not me, then who? You must be mistaken."

"I was just guessing," Sissy Three said.

Fargo didn't believe her. Sisters usually confided in one another. "It's important."

The little one bit her lower lip, then went to say something. But Sissy Two rushed out of the cabin.

"Not a word, you hear? Sissy One will be mad if we tell. We promised her we'd keep quiet."

Butch kneed his mount closer. "You can tell me. You know how much your sister means to me. I love her, and I'm not ashamed to admit it. I'll go fetch her if you'll tell me where she went."

"The last person we'd tell is you," said Sissy Two, and uttered an odd sort of laugh.

"Enough of this." Earl Jagger strode to his roan. "You've wasted enough of my time." He hooked his boot in the stirrup and forked leather. "I'm bringing my cattle in."

"But Sissy One—" Butch protested.

"She's the first girl you've ever kissed and you think she's the one and only female for you. But as soon as your blood cools, you'll see that it wasn't love at all. It was lust."

Butch was appalled. "Pa, how can you say that? I care for her like you cared for Ma."

"Did you ever hear me tell your ma I loved her? No. Once you do that, a woman thinks she has you over a barrel."

"Oh, Pa."

"Sure, I cared for your ma, but I never put her before everything else in my life. That would be plumb ridiculous."

"You didn't?"

"Hell, no. My ranch came first. Then the cows. Then the money they made me. Your ma came fourth, if that."

"Dear God, Pa," Butch said.

Fargo was thinking of Rose and Cletus and Sissy One. Where could they have gotten to? More to the point, who could Sissy One have snuck out to see? "Who else lives in this neck of the woods besides your two families?"

"No one," Earl Jagger said. "I was in these parts first and they came after and there hasn't been anyone since." He lifted his reins. "It won't take me more than half an hour to bring my herd up the valley. You have that long to make up your mind whether you'll stay out of this, and live, or whether you'll try and stop me, and die."

Fargo watched the Bar J outfit ride off. "How do I get myself into these messes?"

"You must have a knack," Sissy Two said.

8

"It's hot," Sissy Two complained. "It's hot and I'm sweaty and I'm tired of walking. I want to go back."

Fargo had the Ovaro's reins in his left hand and was intently examining the ground for sign. "We can't just yet."

"You never should have brought us with you," Sissy Two wouldn't let it drop.

"I couldn't leave you there," Fargo said. Not with their parents missing and the Apaches out for blood and Jagger's outfit about to overrun their homestead.

Sissy Three smiled. "I'm glad you brought us. I like your company. You're the nicest man I ever met."

If that was the case, Fargo figured she hadn't gotten to know all that many. Unbending, he regarded the bleak terrain. They were at the fringe of the mountains to the west of the valley. The ground was hard and did not bear prints well but he had found a few near their cabin that led in this direction and had been tracking them for more than an hour in the blazing heat. He must find the missing Sandses. Either that, or be stuck watching over two small girls.

Sissy Two was gazing toward the end of the valley. "Pa will have a fit when he sees that. He'll kill Mr. Jagger for sure."

The cattle had reached the cottonwoods. From where Fargo stood he couldn't see the spring but it was easy to imagine the scene: the cows jammed tight around and in the water. It would be a miracle if they didn't drink the spring dry.

Sissy Two was a fount of criticism. "You should have stood up to him. You should have stopped him."

"The only way to stop him was for me to kill him."

"So?" Sissy Two clucked in disapproval. "A real friend would do what needed doing. Or is it that you were afraid because there were so many of them? It could be you have a yellow streak."

Fargo was glad he'd never had kids of his own. If this was how some of them behaved, it would take all his self-control not to bend them over his knee and tar their backsides.

"Leave him be, darn you," Sissy Three came to his defense. "He's trying to help us."

"Running from a fight isn't any kind of help. Ma and Pa would have stood up to Jagger."

"Ma and Pa aren't here," Sissy Three said angrily, and then softened with worry. "I'm afraid something might have happened to them."

"Not to our ma. She can handle anyone or anything."

Fargo admired the girl's confidence but she didn't seem to grasp that they were dealing with *Apaches*. "Hush now. I'm trying to think."

"Don't strain yourself," Sissy Two said.

The marks and scuffs of unshod horses led up into the mountains. Fargo made it out to be four altogether. Four Apaches who had snuck in close to the cabin last night, and now were heading for the high rocky fastness few whites ever penetrated. If he was right, they had three captives: both parents, and Sissy One. And now here he was, out to rescue them with two kids along. "I must be half loco," he said under his breath.

"What was that?" Sissy Two asked.

"Nothing. I told you to hush and I meant it."

"You're not my ma or my pa. I can talk as I please."

"I'll remember you said that when you have an arrow

sticking out of your side." Fargo knew he had made a mistake the instant the words were out of his mouth.

Sissy Three blanched and terror etched her face. "You think the redskins got them?"

"I don't know for sure," Fargo hedged.

"The Apaches won't hurt them," Sissy Two confidently predicted. "They're our friends. We gave them our horses, remember?"

Which had to be just about the stupidest thing Fargo ever heard of. But he responded with, "Let's hope you're right."

The land appeared dead, done in by the heat. It was too hot even for lizards and snakes. Save for a solitary buzzard circling high above, they were the only specks of life on the mountain they were climbing. The sun ruled the furnace of its creation in all its fiery majesty.

The chink of the Ovaro's hooves on rock seemed unnaturally loud. There was no wind. Nature seemed to be holding its breath for fear of frying its lungs.

Fargo was so engrossed in searching for sign that when Sissy Three said something, he didn't catch it. "What was that?"

"Why is the world the way it is?"

Fargo looked up. Here they were, in the middle of Apache country, being baked alive, her parents missing, and she asked a question like that? "Ask your ma when you see her."

"I did once."

"Then why ask me?"

"Because she didn't know. She said the Good Lord has His ways, and that's all there is to it. She also said God loves us. But if God loves us, why does God let bad things happen to people?"

"Ask God. Or a parson." Fargo wished he had a bottle of whiskey in his saddlebags.

"I thought you might know, you being so smart and all."

"My sister is smitten with you," Sissy Two said.

Sissy Three whirled on her. "You take that back! I am not."

"Are too."

"Am not."

"Are too."

"Quiet!" Fargo exploded, surprised by his own temper. If this was what parents had to put up with, day in and day out, it was no wonder many married men spent their evenings at their favorite watering hole. It was enough to drive a teetotaler to drink.

"You shouldn't shout," Sissy Two said. "The Apaches might hear you."

Fargo found himself hoping she would step on a rattlesnake. "Not one more peep out of either of you."

Sissy Three giggled. "You sound just like our pa."

"Hell," Fargo said.

Nowhere was there haven from the heat. Nowhere was there a patch of green to break the monotony of the brown. Heat waves rose in shimmering testament to the high temperature. To be abroad for any length of time was to be roasted alive.

Fargo began to cast about for a spot to rest. He regretted bringing the girls. Well, Sissy Three, at least. She shuffled gamely after him, caked with sweat and grime, her stamina sapped. She was a tough little kitten. But if he did not find somewhere soon, he might end up carrying her. Sissy Two could crawl, for all he cared.

Then the mouth of a canyon appeared. Its high walls promised shade and fleeting respite, and Fargo turned toward it, saying, "This way." His throat was so parched, he couldn't swallow any spit.

"Is there water up in there?" Sissy Two asked.

"I doubt it."

"Then we should keep on after my folks. Or is it that you don't want to catch up to the Apaches? Is your yellow streak showing again?"

"I'm obliged," Fargo said.

"For what?"

"Now I know why woodsheds were invented."

The canyon was an oven. Fargo sweltered. His buckskins clung to him like a wet second skin. Not quite half the day was gone yet he sorely craved water and rest. Removing his hat, he mopped his brow with his sleeve. God, what he wouldn't give to be in Montana! he wryly thought.

The youngest was dragging her heels. "If we don't stop soon, my legs will give out."

"Blame your pretty man," Sissy Two said. "He dragged us up here."

"He's only doing what he thinks—" Sissy Three started to reply, and was cut short by Fargo placing his hand over her mouth.

"Not a sound, either of you!"

They looked at him in bewilderment, then both glanced sharply up the canyon. They had heard what Fargo already detected: the faint but unmistakable sound of voices. Men, speaking in low tones. And they weren't speaking English or Spanish.

"Apaches!" Sissy Two breathed, aghast.

Fargo had not paid any attention to the ground since they started up the canyon. Now he did, and was furious with himself. For there, plain as could be, were the very tracks they had followed most of the morning. The Apaches had gone up this exact same canyon.

"What do we do?" Sissy Three whispered.

A good question. Because unless Fargo was mistaken, the voices were coming closer. To his right were scattered small boulders. To his left were gigantic slabs that had broken off the high rock wall ages ago. Some had been smashed to bits. Others were intact and lay in a tangle of massive stones. "This way!" he commanded, and tugged on the reins to hurry the Ovaro along.

For once the middle girl didn't argue.

A pair of slabs in a V shape offered concealment. The open end was toward the wall. Fargo guided the stallion into the space in between, then shucked the Henry from the saddle scabbard and moved back to hunker. He took it for granted the girls would stay with the stallion but he acquired a shadow at each elbow. "What do you think you're doing?"

"Staying close to you," Sissy Two said.

"Go back with my horse."

Sissy Three touched his arm. "I'd rather not, if you don't mind. I'm sort of scared."

Fargo could tell they both were. They wanted to be with him to ease their fear.

"We'll be good," the middle girl promised.

"You better," was all Fargo got out. For the next moment hooves clattered and into view rode two of the four Apaches he had been tracking, both armed with rifles. Young Apaches, Fargo observed. In no great hurry, they rode past the fallen slabs and on down the canyon without once looking back.

"Whew," Sissy Three whispered.

Fargo shared her sentiment. They had been lucky. Neither of the warriors had noticed the Ovaro's tracks, what few there were on the rocky ground. "I'm going up the canyon. Watch my horse for me."

"We want to go with you."

"No."

Fargo rose and worked his way from cover to cover. He went about thirty yards when a feeling came over him that he should look back. Sure enough, the girls were following. He stopped and waited for them to catch up. "Do you two *ever* listen?"

"We're afraid," Sissy Three apologized.

"What if those red devils find us?" her sibling asked. "Without you to protect us, we'd be goners."

"I doubt they'd kill you," Fargo said. But it was small consolation. Their real fate wouldn't be much better: taken to live with a warrior and eventually become his wife. Few white women lasted long in captivity, and those who did were never the same.

"Please," Sissy Three begged. "We won't be a bother. We'll be as quiet as mice and do whatever you say."

Against his better judgment, Fargo motioned for them to follow. Until now he'd never fully appreciated what parents went through, and he had to wonder how in hell they did it.

The canyon curved. Fargo slowed, sank onto his belly, and snaked forward. Two smaller snakes wriggled at his side. He held out an arm to stop them, then dared to look. The canyon floor sloped to a barren shelf, part of which was in the shadow of an overhang. And there, in the shade, were the other two Apaches, squatting beside a small fire that hardly gave off smoke.

Seated with their backs to the overhang were Cletus, Rose and Sissy One. Both Cletus and Rose were tied, wrists and ankles, and gagged. But their oldest, to Fargo's puzzlement, wasn't.

Twisting, Fargo whispered to the girls, "I need to get closer. Give me your word you'll stay right where you are."

"Take us with you," Sissy Two requested.

"No." It would be hard enough for Fargo to get up there unseen.

"We can be as quiet as you or anybody else. We sneak around all the time and our folks never catch us."

Fargo gripped her by the wrist. "I mean it, girl. Try to follow me and you could get them killed."

Sissy Three said, "We'll stay. But what if those other two Apaches come back?"

"Hide there." Fargo pointed at a nearby boulder. "And one of you keep an eye down the canyon at all times. Savvy?"

Both girls nodded.

"I'll give a holler when it's safe for you to come out."

"We'll come running," Sissy Two promised.

The slope was bare save for a few boulders. None were large enough to conceal a grown man. But to Fargo's left was an erosion-worn gully that split the slope from bottom to top. All he had to do was make it there without being spotted. Tensing, he waited for the right moment. It came a few seconds later when one of the Apaches went over to Sissy One and said something Fargo couldn't quite catch. The other Apache was watching them.

His elbows and knees pumping, Fargo crawled toward the gully. He braced for an outcry or a shot, but none came. Pleased at how easy it had been, he slid over the top. He was halfway to the bottom when he realized he didn't have the gully to himself.

Coiled at the bottom was one of the biggest rattlesnakes Fargo had ever seen, and he was sliding straight toward it.

9

Skye Fargo thrust out his free hand, only to have loose dirt cascade from under his palm. He slowed but couldn't defy gravity, not until he was almost to the bottom. In a swirl of dust he finally came to a stop but now he was only half an arm's length from the coiled serpent, and the snake didn't like the commotion. Up came the rattler's head and its tail commenced to rattling. Out darted its forked tongue.

Fargo didn't blink. The snake could strike lightning fast, much too quickly for him to roll out of the way. He couldn't use the rifle with his one hand braced in the dirt, and he couldn't try to draw his Colt when the movement might provoke an attack. All he could do was lie there and wait for the snake to make up its reptilian mind.

Fargo never did like rattlesnakes. He wasn't one of those people who couldn't stand the sight of a snake's wriggling, writhing form. He just didn't like rattlers because they were so damned unpredictable. Where one might strike another might flee. And it didn't help that he always seemed to encounter one when he least could afford to, like now.

Fargo hoped this one would crawl off but it kept on rattling. Its unnerving eyes with their vertical slits were fixed unerringly on his face. Beads of sweat broke out on his brow and his mouth went drier than it already was, which took some doing.

Fargo had good reason to sweat. A bite to the face

or neck would undoubtedly prove fatal. True, not all those who were snakebit died. Every muscle as taut as wire, Fargo waited with bated breath for the damn thing to make up its pea brain what it was going to do.

One of those beads of sweat trickled down Fargo's forehead. He felt it drip over his eyebrow and ever-so-slowly trickle into his eye. The sweat burned like acid. His eyes began to water and he wanted to blink but dared not for fear it would incite the snake.

Then Providence played its fickle hand, and the snake turned and slowly uncoiled, heading up the gully and away from him.

Fargo let out a long breath. Only when the rattler was too far off to bite him did he slide to the bottom and rise into a crouch. That had been too harrowing for his liking. He started up the gully, prudently staying far enough back that the snake paid him no mind.

The rattler was taking its sweet time, forcing Fargo to go slow. He chafed at the delay, worried about the girls. That in itself was a mild revelation, one he preferred not to dwell on.

The rattler veered toward a large flat boulder. There didn't seem to be enough space between the bottom of the boulder and the ground for Fargo to insert a blade of grass yet the snake slipped underneath as neatly and smoothly as you please.

Good riddance, Fargo thought. Staying shy of that boulder, he continued climbing until he was a few yards below the shelf. Then he sank onto his belly and crawled. He remembered to remove his hat before inching his eyes to the rim.

They were still there, the two Apache and their three captives. Cletus was slumped in despair. Rose glared at the Mescaleros, as defiant of them as she was of everyone. As for Sissy One, she looked mad enough to spit nails. Her arms were across her bosom and she was wagging her foot back and forth as if her ankle had come unhinged.

To say Fargo was taken aback by what he learned next was an understatement.

Jabbing a finger at one of the warriors—both were young, Fargo now saw, no more than twenty, if that—Sissy One snapped, "Damn it, Nah-tanh, you can't do this to them. They're my folks!"

"They try stop us," the young warrior answered in passable English. His swarthy features showed no more emotion than the boulder that snake had crawled under. Apaches, Fargo had always thought, would make great poker players except that when they gambled they tended to be reckless.

"But they're my *parents*," Sissy One stressed, almost pleading with him. "They only did what any ma or pa would do."

"Not Shis-Inday mother," Nah-tanh said. "Not Shis-Inday father."

Shis-Inday, as Fargo knew, was what the Apaches called themselves. It meant Men of the Woods. The word Apache—which translated as "enemy"—was bestowed on them by another tribe, and before long everyone was calling the Shis-Inday "Apaches."

"You don't understand," Sissy One said. "Your ways aren't the same as white ways."

"White ways—" Nah-tanh paused, apparently seeking the right word—"strange."

"You keep forgetting I'm white."

"Nah-tanh not forget," the young warrior said, showing a flash of anger. "You much in Nah-tanh's head."

Sissy One smiled but Fargo got the impression the smile was forced. "That's nice to hear. I'm flattered as can be. But that doesn't change the fact that what you've done is wrong. It doesn't change the fact that you've gone too far."

"Too far?" Nah-tanh repeated.

"Yes. You've taken it for granted I'm yours. But that's not how whites do it. A white woman gets to decide who she will be with. A man can't just come and throw her over his saddle. Or his Indian pony, as the case may be."

"Nah-tanh want you."

"I want to live in a mansion and drive in a fancy carriage. We all have things we want."

"Eh?"

"It's nice that you are so fond of me. It's sweet, even. But you're not taking my feelings into account."

The young warrior digested that, then asked, "How you feel?"

"About you? I like you. You've always treated me nice. You brought us game for our cook pot, and you brought me that bracelet that time."

"How you feel on us?"

Sissy One shifted uncomfortably. "That's what I'm trying to explain. There is no *us*. Not in the way you intend. We're friends. We get along well together, even if I'm white and you're red."

"Friends?" Nah-tanh said.

"Just friends, yes."

"Just?" Nah-tanh turned to his companion and said something in their own tongue, said it so fast that Fargo caught only snatches, and few were words he knew. Then Nah-tanh said to Sissy One, "Just not enough."

Fargo thought he understood. The young warrior was fond of her and wanted to take her as a wife, but she wasn't interested.

"It has to be. Because that's all there will ever be between us. I snuck out of the house to tell you that but you dragged me off before I could. And then you went and brought my parents along."

"They try stop us," Nah-tanh said again. He added significantly, "Not kill them for you."

"That's sweet. But it doesn't change anything. Haul me wherever you like, do whatever you like, it won't make me yours, and the first chance I get, I'll light a shuck."

"Shuck?"

"I'll leave you. Or stick a knife between your ribs. But I'll be damned if I'll stay with a man, *any* man, red or white, when I don't want to."

Fargo liked her grit but not her judgment. If she wasn't careful, she was liable to make her Apache suitor mad. And that could prove fatal, both for her and her parents.

Rising, Nah-tanh went over and placed his hand on the top of her head. "You mine."

"I'm nobody's!" Sissy One declared. "Get that through your thick red skull, will you?"

It happened so quickly Fargo had no chance to stop it. The young warrior suddenly had her by the hair, wrenched her head to one side and cuffed her. Not a light blow, either.

Sissy One cried out and grabbed his wrist with both hands, seeking to break his grip, but he was much too strong. "Let go, damn you!"

Nah-tanh yanked her onto her knees and then halfway to her feet, and when she raked her fingernails across his cheek, he cuffed her again, harder than the first time.

The other warrior, with an amused smile, watched their antics.

Fargo didn't think she was in any real danger, not so long as Nah-tanh wanted her for his woman. But if she got him mad enough, so mad he forgot himself, his rage might eclipse his lust.

"Let go, I said!" Sissy One raked her nails again, leaving red furrows in their wake.

Nah-tanh touched his cheek and stared at the blood on his fingertips. He scowled. And when his friend said something in their own tongue, his scowl deepened. With a guttural grunt he threw Sissy One to the ground and his hand dropped to the hilt of a knife at his hip.

The Apache watching them never heard Fargo. He smashed the stock down on the back of the warrior's head and the warrior folded in a heap. Nah-tanh was intent on Sissy One, and Fargo was almost to them when her suitor either heard the soft scuff of his boots or sensed him, and whirled. Instantly, the knife flashed from the sheath, the blade a bright streak. But Fargo sidestepped and slammed the Henry against the side of Nah-tanh's head. Once, twice, Fargo hit him, and Nah-tanh's legs turned to pudding and his knees gave out. Soundlessly, the young warrior pitched onto his face.

"Skye!" Sissy One squealed, and flung herself at him, her warm arms wrapping tight around his neck.

"Are you hurt?" Fargo glanced down the canyon. The other two Apaches could return at any moment and he wanted to be gone when they did.

"I smart some," Sissy One said. "But not so that I can't show how grateful I am." She kissed him on the mouth.

Just then Rose started kicking and moving her arms and making muffled sounds through the gag, which turned out to be a strip torn from her own dress. As Fargo removed it, she spat to one side and then snapped, "About damn time you got here."

"I came as soon as I found out you were missing."

"Is that a fact?" Rose snorted. "As a tracker you would make a great turtle." She rubbed her wrists, which were chafed raw from her struggles.

Sissy One was freeing her father, and the moment his gag was out, Cletus swore a mean streak, ending with, "Damn these stinking heathens! You should have shot them, not just bashed their heads. Give me your rifle and I'll finish what you started."

"No," Fargo said.

"Why the hell not?"

"They're unconscious."

"So? They're Apaches, and the only good Apache is a dead Apache." Cletus pushed his oldest aside and shoved to his feet. "Your rifle or your Colt," he insisted. "It makes no nevermind to me how I do them."

"No," Fargo said again. He had never shot a helpless man in his life and he wasn't about to cross that line.

Rose, for once, took her husband's side. "You saw what they did to us. Trussed us up like lambs for the slaughter and threw us over their horses! They weren't gentle about it, neither. And when I gave them a piece of my mind, they gagged us."

Fargo could well imagine the tongue-lashing she gave them. She was lucky they hadn't slit her throat. "Forget the Apaches. You have other troubles."

Rose stiffened, and raised a hand to her throat. "Sissy Two and Sissy Three! Where are they? Has something happened to them?"

Fargo pointed. Both girls were hurrying up the canyon. "I brought them with me."

Cletus said sourly, "At least you did something right. But what was that about other troubles?"

"Earl Jagger. He's taken over your spring."

"*What?* And you let him?"

"It's not my water." Fargo had forgotten how much of a jackass Cletus could be.

"We let you and your horse drink. We fed you. We gave our permission for you to stay the night. And how do you repay us? You let another man ride up and lay claim to my property."

Fargo was close to hitting him. If not for the girls, specifically Sissy Three, he would have. "I would shut up, were I you."

Some people never took advice. They did as they pleased and didn't care who they offended. Cletus Sands was one of them. He should have done as Fargo told him. But instead he gave Fargo a shove and growled, "I have half a mind to thrash you."

"At last you got a fact right."

"What are you talking about?"

"You have half a mind," Fargo replied, and arced his fist from down near his thigh. He caught Cletus flush on the jaw, the blow driving him up onto the tips of his toes. Another punch to the gut was all it took to bring Cletus down, dazed but twitching.

"Pa!" Sissy One cried.

The smaller girls added yells of alarm.

Rose did nothing, absolutely nothing at all beyond give her husband a look of utter contempt. Yet this was the same woman who had planted roots in the middle of Apache country to save her husband from prison or from an early grave from drinking himself to death.

Fargo smiled to show Sissy Three he was still her friend, the smile freezing on his face when he saw the two warriors who had left earlier galloping toward them.

And the pair had brought friends.

10

Three friends, to be exact, and one of them Fargo recognized. "Get behind me!" he said to the Sandses, and moved to the edge of the shelf. Jamming the Henry's stock to his shoulders, he fixed a bead on the foremost Apache and when they were still some twenty yards out, shouted, "That's close enough!"

The five warriors drew rein. They showed no alarm, but then Apaches were noted for rarely showing emotion. The man in the lead scanned the shelf and his gaze locked briefly on Nah-tanh. Then his dark eyes shifted to Fargo. "You kill them, white-eye?"

"No, Three Ears," Fargo replied. "I hit them on the head. They are very much alive." He chose his words with care. If he could, he'd rather talk his way out of this fix than fight his way out.

Three Ears looked at Rose and her daughters and then at the prone form of Cletus. "You hit him?"

Fargo nodded. "He doesn't know when to keep his mouth shut."

"Him stupid," Three Ears bluntly declared. "Maybe so better you shoot him."

"I don't want to shoot anyone if I can help it. Not unless I'm left with no choice." Fargo had made it plain. Whether blood was spilled was now up to Three Ears.

Inscrutable as ever, the Apache leader just sat there. Most whites branded him a rabid wolf who slaughtered their kind every chance he got. But there was more to the man than the portrait painted by wagging tongues.

For that matter, there was more to Apaches than most whites gave them credit for. To the average white, the average Apache was an unthinking savage who lived only to kill, kill, kill. But the truth was, Apaches rarely did anything without thinking it out first. They were clever. They were devious. They showed flashes of brilliance. To take them lightly, and paint them wrongly, was a mistake.

Fargo didn't share the general attitude. He saw them as they were, and he acted accordingly.

Three Ears might have sat there not saying anything for a good long while but for Rose, who stepped up beside Fargo and declared, "You can't blame this on us. It's Nah-tanh. He came to take our oldest."

"Nah-tanh forget he Shis-Inday," Three Ears said.

Insight struck Fargo. Suddenly the situation took on a whole new meaning. He should have seen it sooner. Apaches never revealed their real names, their Apache names. They believed that to do so gave others power over them. Their real names were always secret. They used Spanish names, or what their name might be in English, but never the actual Apache name. Yet Nah-tanh had revealed his to the Sandses. Specifically, to Sissy One. It was a serious breach of Apache conduct. And it hinted at something deeper.

"You'll let us leave in peace?" Rose asked. "We don't want trouble with your people. We never have."

"You may go," Three Ears said.

"It's a long way back and we don't have horses."

"Take those." Three Ears pointed at the mounts belonging to Nah-tanh and the other warrior Fargo had rapped on the noggin.

"We'll all have to ride double," Rose said to Fargo. She turned and bent over her husband and smacked his cheek, saying, "Wake up, worthless."

Fargo stayed alert. He lowered the Henry but held it leveled at the warriors. Although Three Ears had said they could go, the others might take exception. Unlike some tribes, where the word of a leader was law, Apache warriors were free to do or not do what their leaders decided.

Cletus's usual sour mood had not been improved any by the clout on the jaw and the punch in the gut. He led one of the Apache horses by the reins, muttering and glaring at Fargo and at the Apaches. The girls stayed close to their mother. Once safely past Three Ears and the others, Fargo hurried to where he had hidden the Ovaro, and forked leather. When he emerged from behind the slab, Sissy Two was on a horse with Rose and Sissy Three was riding with her father. That left Sissy One to climb on behind him. She wrapped her arms around his waist and pressed against his back, saying into his ear, "Isn't this cozy?"

Cletus was all for racing back to save his spring but Rose rightly remarked that it would kill the horses in that heat.

Fargo brought up the rear so he could watch their back trail. He tried to ignore the feel of Sissy One's warm body against his but it was hard to do with her breasts pressed so firmly against his shoulder blades. And it didn't help that each time he glanced back, she gave him a sly little smirk that left no doubt what she was up to. Then one of her hands began rubbing his stomach.

"You sure have a nice body."

"Do I?" Fargo was determined to keep a lookout for Apaches and not have her distract him.

"Muscles on top of muscles. Butch Jagger doesn't have nearly as many."

"What about Nah-tanh?"

"The gall of that redskin, trying to steal me like he did. You can never trust an Injun."

"He likes you. Butch likes you. You're the most popular girl west of the Pecos."

"Hell, I'm the only girl," Sissy One declared. "My sisters are too young for that sort of carrying on."

"And you?" Fargo probed. "How much carrying on do you do?"

"Now, now. A lady never tells. But I will say I like to be admired as much as the next gal."

"I would never have guessed."

Sissy One took him seriously. "You're not much good at reading women, are you? I've given you enough looks and hints but you've hardly showed an interest. I was beginning to think you're not partial to females."

"If you only knew," Fargo said.

"Prove it. Take me for a walk when we get back. Somewhere off in the cottonwoods, just you and me."

"You're forgetting Earl Jagger."

"Oh. That's right. Him and his stupid cows. Butch told me that his pa had a wife once but she didn't like cows and didn't take to ranching life and begged Earl to get a job in the city. And do you know what he did? He told her she could go work in a sporting house, for all he cared. If you ask me, anyone who will pick cows over females is a pretty poor excuse for a male."

Fargo had to chuckle.

"Me, I'll never marry. I'd never tie myself to just one man. It would be too boring. Most men are as dull as stumps anyway, and living with them day in and day out only makes a woman realize how little they have to offer."

"Did you learn that from your mother?"

"Truth to tell, I did. Oh, she never came out and said it, but I have eyes, and I see what she puts up with from Pa, and I would as soon slit my wrists as be shackled to a man whose idea of excitement is a whiskey bottle." Sissy One placed a hand on his shoulder and playfully squeezed. "Now you, you're different. You go where you please, do what you want. You're not tied to anyone or anything. I bet you never get bored."

"Town life tends to bore me after a week or two." Usually because he ended up doing the same thing, day after day.

"There. See? You know how I feel. I'll take excitement over boredom every time." Sissy One placed her mouth close to his ear. "Jagger or no Jagger, my invite stands. A wink and a nudge and I'll go off with you."

"What about your father?"

"What he doesn't know won't upset him. And if we do it careful, he won't catch on." Sissy One giggled and gazed at her parents. "I get away with things all the time right under their noses. I'm sneaky as can be when I want to be." So saying, her hand drifted lower.

Fargo felt her cup him. He stirred, as any man would, and when he spoke next his voice was huskier than it had been. "You're about as brazen as they come."

"You like your women brazen. I can tell." Sissy One lightly ran the tip of her tongue across the back of his neck. "How was that? Nice, I bet. There's a lot more in store if you go for that walk with me tonight." She slid her hand along his inner thigh and back to his crotch. "A lot more, handsome."

Between the blazing sun and her fondling, Fargo was hot enough to burst into flame. He grew as hard as iron. He couldn't let on what she was doing, not when now and again Rose and Cletus looked over their shoulders. The youngest, Sissy Three, glanced back once and grinned as if she suspected.

Having his manhood slowly stroked as he rode was a new experience, and one Fargo liked. He wished he could take her then and there, and made a remark to that effect.

"I wish you could, too," Sissy One said wistfully. "There's nothing in this world I like more than that."

"No wonder your folks keep a close eye on you."

"Don't they, though?" she said bitterly. "They've been doing it since I was fourteen. That was the year my cousin taught me all about the birds and bees in our cabbage patch."

"Your own cousin?"

"Oh, he was four or five times removed, as they say.

It wasn't as if he was my brother or anything." Sissy One sighed. "That was the day I learned what life is all about. The day I learned the power a woman has over men."

"Power?"

Sissy One lightly squeezed his pole. "That's right. Power. A man will fall over himself to please a woman who gives him what he wants. She can wrap him around her little finger as she would a piece of string." She chuckled. "A woman who learns to use that power can get anything she wants."

"That doesn't hold for all men."

"True," Sissy One agreed. "But it holds for most. Which is why secretly a lot of women wear the britches in their families. Ma wears the britches in ours but I guess you've already noticed." Suddenly she let go and placed her hand on his shoulder.

The reason was Rose. She had slowed so the Ovaro could come up next to her mount and now she paced him. "You two are talking up a storm back here. What about?"

Sissy Two, riding behind her, snickered and said, "I bet he's sweet on Sissy One. Every other man is."

"Hush, brat," Sissy One snapped. To her mother she said, "I was just saying as how Nah-tanh will leave me be from now on."

"Would that he does," Rose said. "But he's an Injun, and Injuns aren't to be trusted this side of the grave."

"All Indians?" Fargo said.

"Stick up for them if you like, but you'd do well to remember what color you are."

Fargo was so tired of bigots, he could shoot them. It seemed like every time he turned around, he ran into another person who hated for no rhyme or reason other than skin.

"But it's not the Apaches I want to talk about," Rose said. "It's that damn Earl Jagger. He's taken over our water but he'll pay for it in blood. Cletus and me have talked it over and we aim to drive Jagger off."

"Two of you against him and all his men?"

"Our girls will help. We're a family and blood counts for something where we come from." Rose paused. "So do friends. We'd be obliged if you would see fit to throw in with us."

"You want me to do your fighting for you?"

"Did I say that? We fight our own battles. All my girls are good shots. I stuck rifles in their hands when they were barely out of diapers."

Fargo stared. What sort of lunatic was she that she was willing to pit her daughters against grown men in a gun battle? "When lead starts to fly, it's not particular who it hits."

"Are you implying I could get my girls killed?"

"Imply, hell," Fargo said. "I'm telling you flat out. Jagger won't let you push him off. His cows, his ranch, everything he has is at stake. You'll have a war on your hands."

"Spare me a lecture, thank you very much," Rose said indignantly. "And how dare you suggest I don't give a damn about my pride and joys? I care for my girls more than anything. More than I care for Cletus. More than I care for life. More than I care for God."

"Oh, Ma," Sissy One said softly.

"Well, I do. Fargo, here, doesn't understand our kind. He doesn't understand how we do things back in the hills." Rose paused. "Fighting is as natural to us as breathing. We're bred to the feud. Wrong us, and we and our kin will plant you six feet under or die trying." She shook her head sadly. "The biggest mistake I ever made was leaving. I was afraid the law would throw Cletus behind bars. But what I should have done was gone deeper into the hills, gone so far back the law would never find us."

"I wish we had," Sissy One said.

"I've been pondering some, and I've decided that as soon as we settle with Jagger, that's exactly what we'll do."

"Do you mean it, Ma?"

"Why not keep going?" Fargo asked. "I'll go with you as far as the Pecos River."

Rose reacted as if he had slapped her. "You want us to cut tail and run? What kind of man are you?"

Sissy Two said, "I think he's yellow and I told him so to his face. Pay no mind to him, Ma. We'll do whatever you ask us to do, just like always. If you want the Jaggers and their cowhands dead, then we'll kill them for you."

Reaching behind her, Rose patted her middle daughter. "I can always count on you, Sissy Two. Just like I can your sisters. The Jaggers think they can help themselves to our spring but they're about to learn that when you poke a bee's nest, you stir up the whole hive."

Sissy Two laughed and patted her rifle. "I have my stinger handy, Ma. All I need is someone to sting."

"You'll have someone soon enough," Rose assured her. "Before this night is done, the ground will run red with blood."

11

The cattle were still there.

Cows milled about the cabin and grazed on the grass that grew in the vicinity of the spring. They were in the cottonwoods, thickest around the spring. Only one cowboy watched over them. He was leaning against the cabin, looking bored.

The cabin door was open. Apparently Earl Jagger had not only helped himself to the spring; he had helped himself to the cabin, as well, and he and his son and the rest of the hands were inside. From time to time muffled voices and coarse laughter drifted out.

Twilight was falling. Soon it would be dark.

Fargo dreaded the setting of the sun. From his vantage point in a shallow dry wash, he saw the cowboy standing guard yawn. It gave him an idea. "Why don't we wait until they go to sleep? We can disarm them and send them on their way."

On either side of him lay the Sandses, all five of them. Rose was to his left, and she snickered as if he had made a joke.

"Those sons of bitches won't leave our place alive. We aim to kill them and be done with it, not leave them alive to give us more trouble later on."

"But you've decided to head back to Georgia." Fargo's point being that if they weren't going to stay, why kill the Jaggers?

On his right Cletus grunted in disgust. "They've taken

what's ours, and we don't take kindly to that. We don't kindly to it at all."

"Only two of you are armed," Fargo brought up. Sissy Two and Sissy Three had their rifles.

"Three counting you," Rose said. "And we'll get more guns. Don't you worry."

Fargo sighed. He had tried. He'd talked himself half hoarse on the way there but the Sandses refused to heed his advice. They were set on exterminating the rancher and the cowboys, come what may. That was what hill folk did—they feuded—and had been doing since the creation of the hills.

At one point on the ride back Rose had remarked, "I'd be grateful if you would stop badgering us. Our minds are made up and there's nothing you can do."

That was the damnable truth, short of hitting all of them over the head and throwing them over horses. So here Fargo was, about to tangle with a salty cow outfit, all of them armed and no doubt willing to kill for the brand. And on his side, a dried-out drunk with a hair-trigger temper, a woman who refused to bend to any man or God Almighty, and three dirty girls in dirty dresses who did whatever their ma and pa wanted them to do, and that included killing the aforementioned ranchers and cowboys. "Life is too damned ridiculous," Fargo muttered.

"What was that?" Rose asked.

Fargo didn't answer. The sky was rapidly darkening and stars sparkled above. He racked his brain for a way to stop them and was about to draw his Colt and disarm the girls when he realized Sissy Two was no longer in the wash. "What the hell?" he blurted. "Where did your middle girl get to?"

"It's time," Rose said.

Sissy Three was wedging her rifle to her shoulder and taking aim at the cowboy at the side of the cabin.

"She's eleven, for God's sake," Fargo said to her mother.

"You're never too young to kill. And she's only ten and a half. But she's tall for her age."

Then it was Rose and Cletus and Sissy One who were on the move, crawling into the gathering night like Comanches on a raid.

Fargo turned to Sissy Three. "You don't want to do this."

"Sure, I do. Ma needs it done." She didn't raise her cheek from the rifle. "Now be quiet so I can concentrate."

"But you're going to *kill* a man."

"So? I've killed before. It was back to the hills, and we were feuding with thc Crabtrees, and Charley Crabtree, he tried to steal our horses when Ma and Pa and my sisters were gone. So I shot him." Sissy Three smiled. "Ma was real proud of me. Pa said it was the best work I ever did, ridding the world of a Crabtree."

Suddenly Fargo saw their entire family differently. They weren't the fumbling innocents he had imagined. They were a family of killers who lived by a simple code: kill or be killed. "I like you," he said. It came out of its own accord, and he couldn't say why.

"I like you, too."

Fargo kept an eye on the cabin. A lamp or lantern had been lit and a rectangle of light spilled out the door.

A man filled the doorway, his face and front in shadow. Fargo couldn't tell who it was until he spoke.

"Tomorrow we'll cut down some of those cottonwoods and make a corral for our horses. Butch, that's your job. Vern, I want you to take a few of the men and scout around for sign of the Sands."

It was Earl Jagger.

Someone said something inside.

"Like hell we will. We're staying put for as long as this drought lasts, or until the spring goes dry."

Earl Jagger started to turn, and it saved his life. A rifle boomed, and Jagger darted back inside and slammed the door after him.

Sissy Two had fired from somewhere off to Fargo's right.

"She must have missed," Sissy Three said. "Darn her. She knows better than to rush a shot."

The cowboy at the side of the cabin had drawn his revolver and was crouched low, glancing about in confusion. "Mr. Jagger?" he hollered.

Sissy Three shot him.

Fargo swore he heard the lead rip through flesh. He definitely heard the cowboy gasp and saw him slump against the wall, deflating like a punctured waterskin.

"Mr. Jagger! I've been hit!"

Panic was in the man's cry. Fargo almost felt sorry for him. But they had brought this on themselves.

As coolly as could be, Sissy Three fired again.

The cowboy arched his back and his hand flew to his chest. For an instant he hung suspended between life and eternity, and then he keeled over and lay on his side, his legs and arms convulsing.

"That did him," Sissy Three said proudly.

Fargo had been as wrong about these people as he could be. "Don't forget to carve a notch in the stock."

"Why would I do that? That's plumb silly."

More light spilled from the cabin, from the window this time, as the sheet was torn aside. "Travis, are you all right?" Earl Jagger shouted.

From out of the darkness wafted gleeful laughter and Rose yelled, "Your Travis is dead! Just like the rest of you will be."

"Damn you to hell, Rose Sands."

"You're the one who helped himself to what isn't his. You should have stayed on that flea-bitten excuse for a ranch where you belong."

"I'll kill you for this, so help me! Woman or not."

Rose laughed again. She was enjoying herself. "Big talk for someone who doesn't dare show his face at that window."

"I'm no fool," Earl yelled. "No coward, either, as you and yours will find out."

Someone was crawling toward the dead cowboy. It took a few moments for Fargo to realize it was Cletus. Quickly, quietly, Cletus helped himself to the man's revolver, and to a rifle propped against the cabin, and crawled off again.

Rose was keeping the rancher distracted. "We thank you for the cows!" she hollered.

"Over my dead body!"

"Once you are worm food, we'll take them to market and sell them. We'll have a tidy nest egg when we get back to Georgia."

"You're leaving Texas?"

"We sure are. We've had it with this drought and the Injuns and scraping to make ends meet. We never went hungry back in the hills. We never lacked for water, neither. Nor had hostiles to put up with."

Earl Jagger said the same thing Fargo had. "But if you're leaving—" He was quiet a bit; then he called out, "I have a proposition for you."

"It's you or us. There's nothing you can say to change that."

"But if you're leaving, why fight? I'm willing to buy you out. Name your price, and if it's fair, I'll pay."

"Now who is taking who for a fool?" Rose responded. "We've shot one of your hands. You're not about to live and let live."

"All I want is water for my cattle. If the only way to get it without more blood being spilled is to buy your homestead, so be it."

"I don't believe you. You're not the kind to turn the other cheek," Rose told him.

"Damn it, woman. Don't be so pigheaded."

Fargo felt a nudge on his arm.

"Didn't Ma ask you to watch the other side?" Sissy Three brought up.

"You don't mind being here alone?"

"Why would I?" She patted her rifle. "I have this."

Fargo gazed at the dead cowboy, then crawled up out of the wash, his intention to circle around behind the cabin. No shots rang out, and he saw no sign of Cletus, Rose or Sissy Two. He was between the back of the cabin and the cottonwoods and had risen into a crouch when the grass under the trees rustled and a face peered out.

"Hey, handsome, over here," Sissy One whispered.

Fargo went over. She had been busy gathering a pile of broken limbs and sticks. "You're really going to go through with this?"

"Why not? We built it. We have the right to destroy it." Sissy One's teeth showed white in the dark and she placed a hand on his. "But it won't be for hours yet. Ma wants them good and tired. She's hoping most will be asleep. When they come running out, it'll be like shooting ducks in a pond."

"These ducks will shoot back."

Sissy One playfully pinched him. "You are the worst worrier I ever met. I swear, you fret worse than my great aunt, and she worried so much, she gave herself one of those ulcers. Had to drink milk the rest of her life, and she hated milk."

"I'm supposed to watch the other side," Fargo said, and was set to crawl off but she held on to his hand.

"What's your rush? I said it will be hours yet. Besides, I need you to lend a hand. I found a log I want to use but it's too heavy."

Fargo let her lead him into the cottonwoods. Most of the trees weren't any bigger around than his leg, and he wondered where she had found a log so big she needed help. Suddenly something moved close by. Instinctively, he leveled the Henry. But it was only a cow.

Sissy One laughed. "You sure are jumpy."

Cows were everywhere, many bedded down, others standing idle amid the boles.

"Smell the manure? I never could stand that stink."

"How far in do we have to go?" Fargo asked.

"Not much farther." Sissy One threaded through the trees with remarkable ease given how dark it was. She went another twenty feet, then stopped and faced him. "Right here will do."

Fargo should have known. "There's no log, is there?"

"No."

"You brought me out here to have your way with me."

Sissy One grinned. "I surely did." Rising onto her toes, she kissed him lightly on the lips.

"What if your mother or father come looking for you?" Fargo didn't care to be shot while in the act.

"They won't. They're watching the front of the cabin." Sissy One reached up and encircled his neck with her forearms. "You're just about the most skittish man I've ever met."

"Think so, do you?" Fargo had been concerned for the younger girls, but no more.

"There's one way to prove me wrong."

"Are all hill girls like you?"

"If by that you mean we do what we want when we want, and when we've taken a shine to a man, we've got to have him, then yes. I've hankered after you since the moment we met."

Leaning the Henry against a tree, Fargo put his hands on her hips and pressed her against a different one.

"What are you—?"

Her dress was as thin as paper, and under it she wore . . . absolutely nothing. Fargo thrust his hand between her thighs and cupped her mount.

Throwing back her head, Sissy One exclaimed, "Ohhhh! You get right to it, don't you?"

Suddenly a twig cracked behind them. Whirling, Fargo discovered yet another cow. It stood there staring and chewing its cud. He had half a mind to smack it.

"Don't stop," Sissy One said throatily. "This was just starting to get interesting."

"Was it?" Fargo worked his fingers and mashed his chest hard against her breasts.

"Yes. Like that. I like it rough. The rougher, the better. Just don't rip my dress. It's the only one I have and we don't have the material to make me a new one."

"That's too bad," Fargo said in false sympathy. He parted her nether lips and she shivered delectably.

"I hope you won't be a disappointment," Sissy One said.

"Let's find out."

12

Skye Fargo liked women. He liked the feel of them. He liked the smell of them. Most of all, he liked how it felt when he and a woman reached the crest of their lust. It was safe to say he liked that more than he liked just about anything.

So when Sissy One threw down her gauntlet, Fargo rose to the occasion.

Cupping a breast, Fargo squeezed, and squeezed hard. She claimed she liked it rough; he would give her rough. He took her nipple between his thumb and forefinger and pinched it. She gasped, then groaned, and a hungry smile curled her luscious lips.

"That was a nice start."

Fargo didn't intend to listen to her gab the whole time. He molded his mouth to hers, and when her lips parted, slid his tongue between them to swirl the velvet softness. She could kiss, this girl. Some women kissed with all the ardor of a block of ice, but not Sissy One. She put everything she was into her kisses. Her hands were as busy as her lips, her hips grinding against him in rising abandon.

Fargo's other hand was between her legs. He ran his forefinger along her slit, provoking quivers and moans, and then delicately rubbed the tip across her tiny knob. She bit him. She groaned and sank her teeth into his shoulder, biting so deep, it was a wonder she didn't draw blood.

Reaching behind her, Fargo cupped her buttocks. They

were nicely rounded, yet firm. He kneaded one, then gave her other, lower cheek the same treatment. By the time he moved his hand elsewhere, she was panting like a she-panther and impatiently tugging at his pants.

"I want you naked."

"Ladies first," Fargo said, and dug his nails in. She was sensitive down there, and it brought an "Oh!" of pleasure and a thrust of her pelvis. He scraped his nails across her skin and she shuddered.

Sliding his hand around in front, Fargo ran his finger across her wet slit. A kittenish mew issued from deep in her throat as he slid his finger into her womanhood.

Sissy One became a wild woman. She kissed him, she licked him. Her fingers were everywhere, exploring and caressing, her hips swiveling in sensual arousal.

Fargo pumped his finger in and out.

Sissy One threw her head back. Her eyes were shut, her face ecstasy given form. When he rimmed her wet well, she started to cry out but caught herself and bit her lower lip. She was in heaven. Under different circumstances—were they somewhere safe—he was sure she would scream and shriek and carry on deliciously.

Fargo inserted a second finger.

Sissy One planted smoldering kisses on every square inch of his face. She nipped at him as if he were sugary cake. Her lips founds his and she sucked on his upper lip and then his lower one. She began to utter tiny coos and didn't stop.

Fargo slid her dress off over her head. In the starlight she was breathtaking. The swell of her breasts and thighs, the dark triangle of her thatch, the taut bow her body made—she was everything a man could ask for.

The world around them faded. There was Fargo, and there was the hot woman thrashing against him, and that was all. Pleasure was everything, pleasure was king. He tingled with it, throbbed with it, craved more and more of it.

Sissy One tore at his pants, fit to rip them off. She

got his belt undone and tugged, and the next he knew, she dipped at the knees and a wonderfully wet sensation enfolded him. It was his turn to gasp. His turn to make sounds of raw passion.

Fargo's body pulsed to the beat of his desire. His blood roared in his veins. He was on the verge of exploding when he consciously pulled himself back from the brink. He never did like to go over the edge first. Call it silly, call it a male notion, call it what you will, he liked it when the woman gushed first. That was his way, his habit.

Sissy One was talented. You would not have thought a country girl, a girl from the hills, was as good as a seasoned dove or a gilded lovely in a house of ill repute, yet she was. She did things, little things that elicited big gasps, that hinted at uncommon experience. For a brief instant Fargo wondered how it was she was so good at it, and then the pleasure drove rational thought from his mind and left only bliss.

Fargo pulled her to her feet. He spread her legs. He tucked his knees, aligned his member, and rammed up into her. One arm around her waist, he devoted the other to her hard nipples. For her part, she wrapped her legs around his waist, locked her heels, and became a flesh-and-blood piston, rising and falling, rising and falling.

Fargo didn't hold back. He drove in hard, rising onto his toes with each and every thrust. He impaled her again and again and again, transforming her into a tigress. She gave as good as she got, and sometimes when she bit him, she drew red drops. Her nails were claws that left crimson lines. She was wonderful. She was glorious. She was the reason for breathing.

Fargo could have gone on like that forever. But of course they couldn't. There were limits, and they had reached theirs.

As Fargo hoped would happen, Sissy One hurtled over the precipice. If she was a madwoman before, now she was a carnal berserker. She gushed and gushed, drenching him with her honey. Her release brought him over the brink. He went over willingly and soared on satin wings of pure rapture.

At moments like this, nothing else mattered.

But as the old saying went, all good things come to an end, and their delight was no exception. They floated down from the pinnacle, their movements growing slower and slower until finally Sissy One sagged against the tree and Fargo slumped against the soft cushion of her bosom. They were both breathing heavily and caked with sweat.

"That was marvelous," she breathed into his ear. "We'll have to do it again real soon."

Fargo would like that. He would like that very much.

"You're the best I've ever had," Sissy One went on. "You're the best ever, and that's no lie."

Fargo let her think what she wanted. He never thought of himself as anything special.

"You're better than the rancher's son, better than that Apache. They can't hold a candle to you."

The full import of what she was saying sank in. It brought Fargo out of himself, back to the here and now. "You've made love to Butch Jagger and Nah-tanh?"

"Butch only once. He's not much good at it. Clumsy as can be. I suspect I was his first."

"And Nah-tanh?"

"Oh, I snuck out to be with him quite a few times. He's not much for kissing and fondling. He likes to get right to it. But Lordy, does he last! He can go on and on for hours."

"Hell," Fargo said. He stepped back and began putting himself together. His gun belt had slid down around his knees.

"What's the matter? You almost sound mad at me."

"Was it their idea or yours?" Fargo asked as he hiked his belt and made sure his Colt was still in the holster.

"What difference does it make?" Sissy One picked up

her dress and shook it. "I like to make love. They were handy. Just as you were handy. And I don't think you have anything to complain about."

"Now I savvy why Nah-tanh wanted you for a wife. And why the Jagger boy asked you to marry him."

Sissy One laughed. "There's a simpleton if ever there was one. Just because I slept with him, he thinks he's in love. Can you believe it?"

"You've brought a lot of this down on your own head."

"What are you talking about? All I did was sleep with them. And it's not like I sleep with married men like Ma does."

"What?"

"She'll sleep with just about anything in britches. Why do you think my pa took to drink? Why do you think he has the temper he does? Because Ma sleeps around on him. That man he beat to a pulp back in Georgia and almost went to prison for? Ma was carrying on with that fella, and it drove Pa near mad."

"Damn me for a fool."

"What's the matter? It's nothing for you to be upset about. To be honest, I'm surprised she hasn't done it with you. But then she hasn't had the time, what with being took by Nah-tanh and now this business with Earl Jagger." Sissy One giggled. "I suspect she's slept with him, too."

"You're kidding me." But Fargo knew she wasn't. He thought of Cletus. No wonder the man was as prickly as a cactus. Cletus must love Rose, truly love her, and her shenanigans had driven him so deep into the bottle, he still craved liquor to numb the hurt.

Sissy One slid her dress over her head. She smoothed it, fluffed her hair, and smiled. "Anything else on your mind?"

"You and your mother sure set a good example for your sisters."

"Who are you to preach to me? I didn't hear you being so noble a few minutes ago when you and me were swapping spit. It seems to me you're making a lot more out of what Ma and me do than there is."

"Let's go," Fargo said, and turned.

Sissy One grasped his wrist. "Hold on. Explain to me what is going through that handsome head of yours."

"You've brought all this down on yourselves. I wouldn't have any part of it now except for Sissy Three. And I'll be damned if I'll kill for you."

Sissy One put her hands on her hips, her eyes flashing with more than star gleam. "Listen to you. Who are you to judge us? You're forgetting that the Jaggers have taken our home and our water. We didn't start this. They did." She strode past him. "I thought you were our friend but I reckon I was wrong."

Fargo started after her and nearly collided with a cow. He swatted it on the rump and it moved out of the way. When he reached the tree line, Sissy One was nowhere in sight. Crouching, he continued around to the far side of their cabin.

Light came through gaps Cletus hadn't bothered to fill. Squatting, Fargo tried to see inside but all he could make out were shadows. He could hear them, though. Butch Jagger was talking.

"—all I'm saying is we should give it a try. Why spill blood if we don't have to, Pa?"

Earl Jagger gave a snort of derision. "You want *me* to sue for peace. To step outside with a white flag and ask to parley with Rose so we can work this out?"

"Why not at least try? We've already lost one of our hands. I don't care to lose more."

"It will be a cold day in hell before I'll give in to that woman," Earl Jagger said. "I took her for a friend but she stabbed me in the back."

"By not letting us use their spring?"

"What else? Damn, boy, you can be a disappointment. We are in for a fight and I need you with me, heart and soul. But all you do is nitpick and complain."

"I'm no killer, Pa. I'm a cowman."

"So am I, boy. And a cowman worthy of the name puts his cows before all else. Those critters out there are our livelihood. They'll die without that water, and it's up to us to see that they don't. If that means helping ourselves to what's not ours, so be it."

"This couldn't have anything to do with her, could it?"

"Who? That Sissy One you're so fond of?" Fargo heard Butch cough.

"This wouldn't have anything to do with you and Mrs. Sands, would it? I mean, you're not doing this to get back at her, are you?"

Silence lasted for all of half a minute, then Earl Jagger said gruffly, "If you weren't the fruit of my loins, I'd shoot you."

"What? Why?"

"You don't know when to curb your tongue."

"But you always say for me to speak my mind."

"Not at a time like this." Earl swore. "But to set you straight, there's nothing between her and me. And us bringing our cattle here was to save them and no other reason. Satisfied?"

"Don't be mad. But I'm not stupid. I know you saw her a couple of times, just the two of you, and—"

"That's enough. We don't air our personal affairs in front of the hands. Anything more you have to say to me, you can say it when we're alone."

"But it's just Vern and the boys."

"When will you learn?" Earl was angry now. "I did my best to raise you right. To make a man of you."

"And you did a good job."

"No, I didn't. You cling to childish notions. You're too trusting. You are an infant in a man's clothes."

"Oh, Pa. You're—"

"I'm not done. You always think the best of people, even when they are out to stab you in the back. Take that oldest girl of the Sands. Do you really think I'd stand still for you marrying her?"

"Enough, Pa," Butch said. "If I can't talk about you and her ma, you can't talk about her and me."

"That's fair, I reckon. But you better get one thing through your head and not forget it."

"What would that be?"

"No matter what you think of that girl, or how friendly I was with her ma, the Sands refused to help us when we were desperate. They forced this on us. Now it's them or us and it damn well won't be us."

"What are you saying, Pa? That trying to work this out with them is out of the question?"

"Do I have to spell it out for you? We're not letting them drive us off. The Sands and that friend of theirs started the lead-throwing, and they're all as good as dead."

13

Judging by the position of the Big Dipper, Fargo reckoned it was close to two in the morning when things came to a head. He wanted no part of any of it. Both the Sandses and the Jaggers were in the wrong. He stayed only because of Sissy Three, and now, after witnessing her shoot that cowboy Travis in cold blood, he had nothing to tie him there. But he couldn't bring himself to leave. He wanted to see how things played out.

The Sandses ignited the fuse. They had been busy beavers, quietly gathering limbs and twigs and piling them around the cabin. It didn't seem to bother them that they were fixing to burn down their own home.

Fargo felt no urge to warn the Jaggers. Not the father, anyway. The son's only black mark was that he was green behind the ears. That, and he was sticking with his father when he should be shed of the whole scheme to steal what didn't belong to them.

Fargo was lying in the grass, his chin on his forearm, when a shadow crept out of the dark and roosted beside him. He didn't bring the Henry up. He could tell by the way the person moved—and the slight swish of her dress—who it was. "Come to spell me?"

"To warn you," Rose said. "We're about to start the dance and you need to be ready."

"For what?"

"To kill them, silly. Once the flames are high enough, they'll bolt like scared rabbits. We'll shoot them down as they come out."

"I'm not shooting anyone."

"Why the hell not?" Rose demanded, and then stared intently at the cabin. "Are my eyes playing tricks? You haven't piled any wood."

"None whatsoever."

"I told you what I wanted, didn't I? To light all four sides at once to make sure they don't escape."

"You'll have to make do with three unless you want to gather wood and light this side yourself."

Rose regarded him as she might a bug that had crawled out from under a rock. "What's gotten into you? I thought you were on our side."

"I'm on my own side."

The dark hid Rose's expression. "This is a fine how do you do. We were hospitable to you, and this is how you repay us."

"Save your breath." Fargo imagined her with Earl Jagger, and God knew how many others. Yet she acted the part of the aggrieved wife and blamed their plight on her husband.

"Very well. But I warn you. Stay out of this. Don't side with them against us, or I'll kill you myself. Honest to God I will." With that, Rose angrily wheeled and stalked off.

Rising, Fargo ran to the cabin and pressed his ear to a gap. From within came loud snoring. He crept to the front corner. An inky shape was bent low over the piled branches. A flame flared and gave birth to more. They quickly grew, and in their light Fargo saw Rose, her face agleam with bloodlust. She was ruthless, this woman.

Nodding in satisfaction, Rose scooted into the darkness. The flames spread rapidly, fanned by the night wind. Some of the boards caught, giving off smoke and crackling loud enough to wake the dead. Or those asleep inside.

Fargo gave the cabin a hard thump. Then another.

"Wake up! Wake up! Does anyone smell smoke?"

It sounded like the cowhand called Vern.

Fargo ran to the rear of the cabin. Sissy One had already lit her pile and flames were climbing toward the roof. Sissy Two had probably done the same on the other side.

"Fire!" someone bawled within. "They've set the place on fire!"

"They wouldn't dare!" Earl Jagger bellowed. "It's their home!"

The next second Rose shouted, "Can you hear me in there?"

"We can hear you, you bitch!" was Earl's reply.

"Throw out your rifles and your six-guns and come out with your arms in the air and we'll let you live."

"Like hell, you will! You just want an excuse to disarm us so you can blow us to hell."

"You have my word!"

Earl Jagger told her what she could do with it.

"You never did know how to treat a lady nice!"

"Show me one and I will."

It was like listening to children argue. Fargo retreated far enough to be safe, he hoped, from stray slugs. By now flames were eating at the roof. The front wall was half consumed. Only the wall on Fargo's side was untouched.

Suddenly the front door was jerked open, framing a cowhand. He had a revolver in his hand and panic on his face.

"Bob, don't!" Earl hollered.

But the man had endured all the smoke and flame he was going to, and he broke from the cabin at a full run. But he had only taken a few strides when a rifle cracked and he jerked as if punched but didn't go down. Spinning, he snapped a shot in the direction of the shooter—which happened to be toward the dry wash. The cowboy ran on, only to be brought up short by a shot from in front of him that cored his brain.

"I got him!" Cletus crowed. "Did you see me, Rose? I blew the top of his head clean off!"

"Shut up, fool!"

If Fargo had the tally right, that left five inside: Earl, Butch, the two-gun man called Reese, the cowboy named Vern, and one other. The odds were even now.

The Sandses commenced firing at the walls, hoping, evidently, to drive the rancher and cowboys out that much sooner. And it worked, but not in the way they expected.

Fargo was nearest the unlit side, and only he heard the *thwack* of an axe biting into wood. More blows ensued, not all from an ax. Inside, Earl and company were attacking the unlit wall, battering and hacking with whatever was handy. And since the wall wasn't well constructed, since it consisted of old boards from the covered wagon and thin cottonwoods, in no time at all a hole appeared and swiftly expanded.

From over on the left came a bellow from Cletus. "What's that noise? Rose, you hear that?"

"They're trying to break out! Quick! The south side of the cabin! Damn that Fargo anyhow!"

Figures rose and sprinted through the night.

Fargo wasn't one of them. He stayed on his belly, the Henry at his side. No matter what, he wasn't taking part.

The hole was now wide enough and high enough that a man could duck through it, and that's what a cowboy did, followed instantly by another. Another moment and Vern, Reese and Butch were all out, and Butch was helping his father, all of them coughing from the smoke.

Then a rifle cracked, and another, and a cowboy went down.

Reese sprang past the others and drew his Smith and Wessons, as slick a two-gun draw as Fargo ever saw. Reese fired from the hip, shooting at gun flashes, and God, the man was fast. He pinned the Sandses down long enough for Earl and Butch and Vern to fly to safety and then he backed after them, firing as he went.

Fargo was impressed.

The shooting stopped. Silence fell, save for the roar

of the fire. The cabin was nearly entirely engulfed, flames rising high into the sky.

Fargo waited, and when he was sure Jagger and the hands were gone, he rose and cautiously sought the Sandses. He avoided the wide circle of light cast by the fire. Low voices and a sob drew him to a knot of clustered figures. A sinking feeling came over him when he saw that four of them were gathered around a fifth who was prone on the ground. He hurried over and nearly paid for his haste with his life when Cletus swung toward him and pointed a six-shooter.

"Oh. It's only you."

Fargo went up to the body. "Damn," he said.

It was Sissy Two. A slug had cored her just above an eye and part of her eyelid and eyebrow were gone. Her body was contorted in death, her teeth bared as if she were about to take a bite out of her killer.

Sissy Three and Sissy One knelt on the other side of her. Sissy Three was crying.

"This is your doing," Rose Sands said.

"How is that again?"

"This is your fault. You didn't set your side of the cabin on fire as you were supposed to. They were able to break out. That gun hand—Reese, I think his name is—he sprayed lead, and one of his shots took my girl here." Rose looked up, her eyes glistening with the tears she was holding back. "It's your fault, you son of a bitch. I will see you dead for this."

To Fargo's surprise, Cletus said, "Now, Rose, you can't blame him. He told you he wouldn't take part. You should have lit the fire yourself."

"Are you blaming *me*?"

"I'm only saying, is all."

"How dare you, Cletus! My girls mean more to me than anything. More to me than life. More to me than *you*."

"Don't get hysterical on me," Cletus said.

Rose pushed to her feet and grabbed hold of the front

of his shirt. "Hysterical? *Hysterical?* I'll give you hysterical! I'll take this rifle to your empty head, is what I'll do."

Cletus tore her hand loose and angrily shook a fist. "Don't talk to me like that, damn your female hide! I'm your husband and you'll treat me with the respect I deserve!"

"Which is absolutely none."

Fargo couldn't believe it. There their daughter lay, freshly dead at their very feet, and they were squabbling again. They had forgotten her. For all their talk of love, all they ever thought about was themselves. As for it being his fault, he refused to accept that. Cletus was right. He *had* told her he wouldn't help burn the cabin. Hell, he had tried to talk them out of the whole thing. It was Rose who came up with the idea. It was Rose who gave the others their orders, like a general commanding her private little army. If anyone was at fault, it was her.

Cletus was giving his wife a piece of his mind. "When this is over, I have half a mind to leave you. I've put up with so much over the years. But this is the last straw."

"You've put up with a lot?" Rose responded. "*I've* had to put up with a lump of a husband who never has amounted to much and likely never will because he's lazy and brainless to boot."

"You're as lazy as me," Cletus said. "You're so lazy, you couldn't be bothered to come up with names for our babies. You named them all the same except for the numbers so they'd be easy to remember."

"You never heard them complain. And if we're going to list faults, I could go on for an hour about yours. You're sure not the man I thought you were when I married you. Every time life gets hard, you sulk in a bottle. Me, I deal with problems. I sweep them out of the way and get on with my life."

"You *are* the problem, damn you. You and your carrying on with other men when you think my back is turned. But you're right about one thing. If I was the man you wanted me to be, I'd have shot you years ago."

Fargo wanted to punch them both. "So much for your daughter."

They glanced at him, and Rose blinked and said, "What was that you just said?"

"Sissy Two is dead. *Dead.* And you two stand there bickering. You disgust me."

"Here, now," Cletus said.

"Don't make me madder than I already am," Rose warned. "Yes, Sissy Two is gone, and I hold you to blame. You'd be smart to fight shy of me for a while."

"It's too bad that's not you lying there," Fargo said, and wheeled before he slugged her. He had taken half a dozen steps when he was startled by a warm hand clasping his.

"Can I be with you?" Sissy Three asked, sniffling.

"Sure."

"She was my sister. She picked on me a lot, and didn't always treat me nice, but I'll miss her."

"That's natural," Fargo assured her.

"For all the spats we had, I cared for her. I loved her. Now she's gone. She's gone forever, and I hurt."

Stopping, Fargo faced her. "I'm sorry." What else was there to say? He'd never had to comfort a girl her age before.

Suddenly Sissy Three dropped her rifle and threw herself at his legs. She buried her face against him and broke into great, racking sobs, her whole body shaking. She cried and cried and cried, and Fargo let her. He didn't know what else to do.

But the whole time Fargo was uneasy. He continually probed the night for Jagger's bunch. He wouldn't put it past Earl Jagger to sneak back and try to catch the Sandses unaware. At any moment the dark might erupt with more gunfire. But his worry proved groundless. No shots boomed, and eventually Sissy Three stopped crying and stepped back, her face slick with tears and snot.

"I'm sorry."

"No need to be." Fargo patted her shoulder. "It was good to let it out. Now you'll feel a little better."

"I'll never feel like my old self ever again," Sissy Three said softly. "And I won't rest until blood has paid for blood."

"How do you mean?"

Sissy Three looked up. Gone was the little girl, the innocent child. The light from the burning cabin bathed a face as hard as any Apache's. "I'm going to kill them for what they did, Mr. Fargo," she declared. "I'm going to kill every last one of them."

14

Fargo figured the cowboys had made for their horses, and he was right. At first light he tracked them, the Sands family glued to his heels. The footprints led to a small clearing in the cottonwoods to the south of the spring. Holes showed where picket pins had been.

"Why'd they keep their horses here and not close to the cabin?" Sissy One wondered.

"No doubt to hide them from us," Rose speculated. "Maybe they thought we'd run them off."

Fargo roved the clearing, his brow puckered. He checked twice to be certain he was reading the sign right.

"Well, which way did they ride off?" Cletus impatiently asked.

"They didn't."

"What are you trying to pull? Their horses are gone."

"They didn't ride off. They walked." Fargo dropped to one knee to inspect a faint impression. "Someone else got to their horses before they did."

"Who?" Rose sounded skeptical. "It wasn't us. Who else is—" She stopped and jerked up the rifle she had taken from a dead cowboy. "It must have been the Apaches."

"The Apaches," Fargo confirmed. The tracks showed where Earl Jagger and the other three had walked about in confusion. *Stomped* about would be more like it for Earl Jagger, who must have been as mad as a bee-stung bull.

"Three Ears, you think?" Rose asked.

"Impossible to say." Moccasins left no more than scrapes and scuffs only the best of trackers could read. "But there were seven or eight of them."

"That's more than we saw at the canyon," Cletus said.

Rose nodded. "This complicates things."

As far as Fargo was concerned, her assessment was short of the mark. What with the drought, and Rose and Sissy One having slept with everything in pants, it went beyond complicated.

"This is good, though," Cletus said. "We can follow them on horseback and catch them in no time."

"Unless the Apaches took our horses too, Pa," Sissy Three said.

Fargo hadn't thought of that. He was up and out of the cottonwoods at a full sprint. They had left the Ovaro and the Apache mounts down the dry wash, ground hitched so they wouldn't stray off. He swore at himself for not checking on the stallion sooner.

The Sandses hurried after him, Rose yelling for him to slow down.

Fargo ran faster. He reached the wash and flew to the bottom and then along its winding course until he came to the spot where their horses had been.

The Ovaro and the others were gone.

Stunned, Fargo cast around for sign and found more scuffs and scrapes and one clear moccasin print. "Damn me," he said, and kicked the ground in anger. Getting the Ovaro back from Apaches wouldn't be easy. It wouldn't be easy at all.

The Sandses got there, huffing and puffing and red in the face. Cletus blistered the air with cuss words until Rose hushed him.

"It's not as if they were our own animals. True, we could have used them, but it's no great loss." Rose looked at Fargo. "Except for your pinto."

"What do we do now, Ma?" Sissy One asked.

Sissy Three said, "We go after Earl Jagger and we kill him."

Fargo thought again of the sweet little girl who had clasped his hand. "Spilling their blood won't bring your sister back."

"No, but it will make me feel better."

"We're wasting time," Rose said. "Let's drink our full at the spring and light out after them."

"I wish our waterskins hadn't burned with our cabin," Sissy One remarked. "It's going to be another scorcher."

"A little thirst won't hurt us," Cletus, of all people, said. "We have a feud to finish."

No one suggested that Fargo stay behind. They needed him. He was the only one who could track.

Cows were thick at the spring. Fargo had to swat some to get them to move. When he hunkered to drink, he found that the water had been god-awful muddied, to the point where he was loathe to dip his hand in. But he did. Already he was sweating badly, and the sun was barely an hour high.

"Damn these critters anyhow," Cletus complained. "I'd as soon shoot every last one of them."

"No you won't," Rose said sternly. "Think of how much they'll fetch us when we get them to market."

"They're Jagger's, not ours."

"Husband, sometimes you are dumber than a stump. If we kill Earl Jagger, then these cows belong to whoever claims them. And that will be us. We'll hold them here until the drought breaks or the spring starts to go dry, then drive them to the nearest town and sell them."

"That's a great idea, Ma," Sissy One said.

Fargo didn't point out that the law would call that murder and stealing. But then, there wasn't any law west of the Pecos.

High-heeled boots made tracking easy. The heels left clear marks even in hard-packed dirt. Fargo made good time the first hour or so. Then the heat began to sap their vitality and they slowed to a walk to conserve their energy.

Cletus mopped his forehead with his sleeve and

squinted up at the yellow orb that dominated the blue vault of sky. "It never got this hot back to home. I can't wait to have Georgia soil under my feet. We never should have left."

"We did what we thought was right at the time," Rose said. "Don't beat yourself with hindsight."

"When we go back things will be different. Give your word that you won't sleep around and I'll give mine not to drink. We'll be happy again, like we were when the girls were little."

"I promise," Rose said.

Fargo wondered who was fooling who. He pulled his hat brim lower against the sun and gazed into the distance, knowing it was too soon to spot Earl Jagger but hoping anyway. Presently he acquired a second shadow.

"Mind if we talk?" Rose asked.

"Just so long as your husband doesn't think I'm trying to get up your dress."

Rose chuckled. "I want to thank you for what you are doing. From the bottom of my heart."

"I'm sorry I ever stopped at your place."

"No need to be mean. None of this is our fault. It's been building up for a while and just happened to come to a head when you showed up."

"If you want to pretend, you go right ahead. But don't expect me to believe the lies you tell yourself."

Rose was silent a spell. Then she said, "You're not like most men. You come right out and say what's on your mind. So I'll come right out and say what's on mine." She looked at him. "Last night you wouldn't help us burn our cabin. Because of you, Jagger got away. Because of you, that Reese shot Sissy Two."

"Don't remind me."

"What I want to know—what I need to know—is whether you will help us this time, or whether you'll sit on your hands and do nothing again."

"I'll take it as it comes," Fargo said.

"What does that mean? Will you or won't you? Because if you won't, I don't want you anywhere near when the lead starts to fly."

"I'm not your husband. You don't tell me what to do."

Rose colored and hefted her rifle but didn't swing. "God, you make me mad. But suit yourself. And understand one thing. I don't blame Earl Jagger for Sissy Two. I don't even blame Reese all that much since he was firing blind into the dark. No. I blame you. You've cost me a daughter, and I won't ever forgive you for that, not this side of the grave."

Fargo went on walking.

"Say something, damn you."

Fargo was about to but he stopped dead in his tracks. The ground was pockmarked by the marks of heavy hooves, with clods of earth scattered here and there. Horses, a lot of horses, had passed that way, following the same footprints he was following. Some of the horses had been shod. Some hadn't.

"What's this?" Cletus asked.

"Apaches," Fargo said. The shod horses were behind those that weren't, which suggested they were being led. He recognized one of the horseshoes. "The ones who stole my pinto."

"Three Ears, you think?" Cletus gazed anxiously about. "Why can't he leave us be?"

"This is his land," Rose said.

Cletus swore. "Listen to you. Defending that red devil. Next you'll be telling me that we should have had him over to supper a few times."

"You say the damnedest things."

Fargo shut out their bickering. He walked faster, eager to reclaim the Ovaro, but soon the heat made him slow again. He wryly promised himself that once he was done here, he'd head for somewhere cool. Montana, maybe. Or the North Pole.

"What are you grinning about?"

Fargo glanced down. "Do you still feel the same as you did last night?"

"About what? Killing the Jaggers for what they did to my sister? Need you even ask?" Sissy Three said.

"You're too young to be killing people."

"How old do you have to be? I can hold a rifle and squeeze the trigger, and that's all it takes."

Fargo disagreed. Some people couldn't kill another human being if their life depended on it. They didn't have it in them. It took more than the will to do it. It took a special grit, deep inside.

"Look yonder!" Sissy Three suddenly exclaimed, pointing.

At first glance it looked like a herd of wild horses. Only some had saddles. All told there were nine Apache horses plus the mounts that belonged to Earl Jagger and his men and a splendid black and white stallion that tugged at the rope that held it in an effort to reach Fargo.

"Well, I'll be!" Rose said, and started forward.

"Not so fast." Fargo held out an arm, stopping her. "Get down, all of you." Scouring the stark terrain, he did the same.

"What are we waiting for?" Rose criticized. "They're there for the taking."

"It could be a trick," Fargo warned her. Apaches liked to set out bait to lure in the unwary.

"I don't see anyone," Rose said. "I say we rush over and get them. We'll strand those red devils afoot. See how they like it."

It wouldn't make a difference, Fargo reflected. Apaches could travel fifty miles or more a day on foot. "Stay put while I go have a look-see."

"Nothing doing. I'm going along," Rose informed him. To her husband she said, "Keep the girls here with you. And don't let anything happen to them. Losing one child is enough sorrow to last me a lifetime."

"You can count on me," Cletus said.

"No, I can't. I wish I could. But you have proven worthless, and it will take some doing to convince me you've changed."

Fargo crept toward the horses. Boulders and scrub brush offered plenty of cover. He nearly jumped at a slight sound but it was only a lizard scuttling out from under one boulder to another.

"Where are they? I don't see them anywhere."

"Quiet." Fargo was wondering the same thing. Beyond the horses lay more open land, save for the boulders. Or was that a ridge line he spied?

"Don't tell me what to do. I don't let my husband boss me around and I sure as blazes won't let you."

"Has your husband ever hit you on the jaw?" Fargo asked. That shut her up.

Many of the horses had raised their heads. Fargo half dreaded they would whinny and stamp and alert any nearby warriors.

He had to pass several Apache mounts to reach the Ovaro and one of them tried to kick him but he nimbly sprang aside. The Apaches had used rope taken from the saddles of the cowboys to tether the horses, and it was the work of a few moments for Fargo to unsheathe his Arkansas toothpick and cut them free. He slid the Henry into his saddle scabbard and climbed on the Ovaro, glad to have the stallion under him once again.

"No sign of the Apaches," Rose said. Turning, she beckoned to her family and they came on the run. "Pick an animal and get on," she instructed them. "We have to get out of here while the getting is good."

Cletus was the last to try and mount. His horse was giving him a hard time. He had hold of the reins and the saddle horn but the horse shied each time he raised his foot to the stirrup. "Stand still, damn you."

"Pick another," Rose said.

"I like this one. I haven't ever owned a roan before."

"We don't have time for this, damn it."

Cletus managed to hook his foot but the horse pranced to one side and he couldn't pull himself up.

Fargo made the mistake of watching Cletus and not staying alert to their surroundings. Too late, he registered swift movement out of the corner of his eye. He went to shout a warning just as an Apache launched himself at Cletus's back and slammed Cletus to the ground.

"Pa!" Sissy One shouted.

Sissy Three screamed.

Fargo swooped his hand to his Colt. He saw Sissy One point at something behind him and open her mouth to yell, and then a two-legged battering ram slammed into the small of his back and he was unhorsed. He landed hard on his stomach and the breath whooshed out of his lungs. A knee gouged his spine. The next instant his head was jerked back and a knife flashed before his eyes.

The Apache was about to slit his throat.

15

Frontier life was rife with perils. The mountain and prairie were home to a host of savage men and fierce beasts, and the sun-bleached skeletons of those they preyed on would fill the Grand Canyon. Fargo survived that deadly cauldron of kill or be killed because he had learned early on that when his life hovered on the brink, he must strike hard and he must strike fast or he wouldn't live to see the next dawn.

Accordingly, even as his head was jerked back and the gleaming blade flashed before his eyes, Fargo was in motion. Twisting and rolling, he slammed into the Apache's leg. It caused the warrior to stumble and the blade to miss Fargo's throat by a whisker. Surging up, Fargo drove his fist into the Apache's groin and was rewarded with a grunt of pain. The warrior staggered, his grip slackening. In a blur Fargo drew his Colt, jammed the muzzle against the warrior's middle and blasted two swift shots.

Surprise lit the Apache's dark eyes, fleeting and final, and he clutched his belly and toppled.

Fargo whirled.

Cletus was down, flat on his back and struggling mightily to stop another warrior from burying a knife in his chest. Rose leaped to help him and was flung violently aside. Then it was Sissy One's turn but she fared no better.

That left their youngest.

Sissy Three hurled herself at the Apache and jammed her rifle against his neck.

Once again, the warrior swatted her aside. Or tried to. For when his knuckles struck the barrel, it jarred Sissy Three and her finger closed on the trigger and the rifle went off.

The slug ripped clear through the Apache's neck. He raised his knife to stab her, and Fargo took quick aim. But there was no need to shoot. The warrior was dead on his feet. Eyelids drooping, blood misting in a geyser, the Apache keeled forward and would have fallen on Sissy Three had Fargo not taken a long bound and snatched her out of the way.

Rose and Sissy One were picking themselves up.

Cletus, though, hadn't moved. He couldn't. Scarlet welled from just below his sternum. His mouth moved but all that came out was a whine. Then he gasped and cried out, "Rose! My sweet Rose!"

Flinging herself beside him, Rose pressed a hand to the wound. "Hold on! Maybe it's not that bad. Maybe we can save you."

Both daughters were horror-struck.

Fargo began replacing the spent cartridges in his Colt. He had seen a lot of wounds, and nine times out of ten he could tell when a wound was fatal and when it wasn't. Cletus Sands was a goner.

"Rose! I'm so weak. I can hardly breathe."

"Don't die on me, damn you! For once do something right!" Rose bunched his shirt up over his chest and stared appalled at the Apache's handiwork. "Dear Lord, no."

"Rose? Can you hear me?" Cletus clutched at empty air, and Rose grasped his hand in both of hers. "Why is it so dark?"

"No, no, no, no."

"Say something, Rose. I can't hear you. I can't hear anything. It's like a tunnel, Rose. A long black tunnel, and I think there's—" Cletus arched his back, opened his mouth wide and died.

"Pa!" Sissy Three fell to her knees and grabbed his other hand. "Don't die on us, Pa!"

Fargo was thinking of their own hides. The other Apaches were bound to have heard the shots. He inserted the last cartridge and spun the cylinder, ensuring he had six pills in the wheel.

"He's gone, little one," Rose said to her youngest.

Sissy Three threw herself across her father and broke into racking sobs. "Please, God. Not him. Not my pa."

"We don't have time to mourn," Rose said, pulling on her arm.

"No! Leave me be!"

"There are more Apaches out there, girl. We've got to skedaddle. Come along, now."

Sissy Three broke free. "Stop it, Ma! Go if you have to, but I'm not leaving him."

"He's dead, little one. Look at his chest. It's not moving." Rose again tried to pull her to her feet. "Come on."

"No!"

They couldn't afford the delay. Fargo hooked his arm around Sissy Three's waist and tore her from her father. She fought him, kicking and bucking, as he swung her onto the nearest horse. Then he forked the Ovaro.

"Pa!" Sissy Three shrieked.

Rose was climbing on another animal. Sissy One had a dun's reins but the dun was backing away.

"Hurry," Rose urged.

Fargo shared her worry. He suspected the rest of the Apaches had been closing in on foot on Earl Jagger, but the racket was bound to bring them back on the run. To help Sissy One, he reined the Ovaro alongside the dun and snagged the bridle. With him to hold the horse still, she was in the saddle in seconds.

Rose swatted the horse Sissy Three was on and they trotted back the way they came.

Fargo wasn't about to leave the other horses there for

the Apaches. A whoop and a holler weren't enough to so he fired into the air. Thankfully, the horses stayed bunched together.

A glance over his shoulder revealed stick figures in the distance. Three Ears would get there too late to do anything. As for the Jaggers and the cowboys, they might be dead. If not, maybe they would make it back to their ranch.

The horses were tired and easy to manage. Fargo had no trouble other than a mare that tried to bolt but he was alert and promptly drove her back among the rest.

Rose was holding up surprisingly well. She hadn't shed a single tear for her dear, departed husband. That might change later when she was alone, but somehow Fargo doubted it.

The heat fried them but Fargo didn't stop to rest. He pushed on until they reached the spring. As usual the cows were clustered close to the water but the horses shouldered through.

Fargo sat with both hands on his saddle horn, his sweaty body bent in fatigue, while the Ovaro drank. He wanted a drink, he wanted one badly, but he was watching their back trail.

Rose had climbed down and was splashing water on her face. "I swear. I'll never take water for granted again."

Sissy One waded out up to her waist, squatted, and closed her eyes in ecstasy. "I could stay in here forever."

"Poor Pa," Sissy Three said. Like Fargo, she was still on her horse. "I miss him already."

"Don't get all weepy on me," Rose scolded. "He's gone. We deal with it and we get on with life."

"I thought you loved him, Ma."

Rose stopped splashing to glare. "Of course I cared for him. I stuck by him all these years, didn't I? I put up with his drinking and his laziness. If that's not love, I don't know what is."

"You haven't cried," Sissy One said.

"Hellfire, girl. Some of us like to shed our grief in private. I'll shed tears later. Trust me."

Fargo didn't think she would. The more he learned of Rose, the more convinced he became that her notion of love had more to do with a poke than the heart. "We leave at sundown," he announced.

They looked at him as if he were loco.

"To where?" Rose asked.

The way Fargo saw it, the wise thing to do now was to get them to a fort. The army would protect them, and might even give them vouchers to defray part of the expense of returning to Georgia. The two nearest posts were Fort Stockton, to the east, and Fort Davis, to the south. Stockton was closer to the Pecos River but it was also considerably farther than Davis, and in that heat every mile counted. "We're heading for Fort Davis. And we're taking the stock with us."

Established not quite seven years ago, Davis was built to protect whites from the ravages of the Apaches and Comanches. It was named after Jefferson Davis, who was secretary of war at the time. The 8th Infantry were stationed there, as tough a bunch of soldiers as the army could boast of.

"What if we don't want to go?" From Rose.

"You've lost your husband. You've lost your cabin and everything you own. You're caught in the middle of a drought, with Apaches on one hand and a rancher who hates your guts on the other. Why the hell *wouldn't* you?"

Rose had no answer to that.

"Get what rest you can. As soon as the sun sets, we start out."

Now it was Sissy One who had an objection. "But the horses and the cows won't make it. Not when there's no water to be had."

"Some will," Fargo said. "And we might find water along the way." He knew of a few streams and tanks. Most were probably dry but he would chance it.

"Enough that if you sell them, you'll have money to start over when you get back home."

"You would do this for us?" Rose asked with obvious feeling.

Fargo was doing it for the youngest. He wanted Sissy Three out of there before she wound up like Sissy Two. He never had much to do with kids. They tended to get on his nerves. But he liked her, he liked her a lot. She was sweet and trusting—and could kill a man without batting an eye. If she was twenty years older, she'd make a fine companion. He shook his head at the thought, amused with himself.

"What?" Rose asked.

"Nothing." Fargo dismounted. There was no sign of pursuit. Yet. But Three Ears wasn't about to let them get away, and Apaches, although on foot, could cover ground almost as rapidly as a white man on a horse.

Hunkering, Fargo drank. The water was brown but he didn't care. He cooled his face and neck by dipping his palms in the water and letting the water trickle over his skin. The sensation was wonderful. As he lowered his arms again someone bumped his elbow.

"We have until sunset, you said?" Sissy One asked.

"So?"

"The sun won't go down for hours yet."

Fargo had to chuckle at how her mind worked. "You'll need all the rest you can get. We won't stop until dawn."

Sissy One lowered her voice so her mother and sister couldn't hear. "I can spare a half hour. That is, if you're interested." She grinned and winked.

"Now?"

"Why not? Ma and sis will be asleep. We can walk off a little ways but still be near if they need us."

"Is that *all* you think of?"

"Pretty much." Sissy One put her hand on his leg under the water, and squeezed. "Blame yourself. You're the best lover I ever had."

If Fargo lived to be a hundred, he still wouldn't understand women. But he had to admit, he liked the idea. The swell of her bosom against her soaked dress, the way the dress clung to her when she moved, were enough to tempt any man. And, too, it would help him relax and rest for the ordeal ahead. "We'll wait until they're sleeping."

Sissy One nodded and winked again and then sashayed out of the spring. She was lucky she didn't throw her hips out of the joint, the way she swung them from side to side.

Fargo pulled the Ovaro from the spring. The stallion had enough, almost too much. He was undoing the cinch when a hand fell on his shoulder.

"I haven't thanked you for all you've done for us," Rose said.

"No need."

"You don't think much of me, do you?"

"It's not my place to judge." Long ago Fargo had learned to take people as they were.

"Be honest. You think my sleeping around brought all this on. That if I'd been true to Cletus, he wouldn't have turned to drink and got in trouble with the law, and we wouldn't have come to Texas and he would still be alive right now."

Fargo looked up. "Out of your mouth, not mine."

Rose's lips pressed thin, and she coughed. "All right. I admit it. I am partly to blame. But I never thought it would come to this."

"We never do."

"I'll have to live with the memory of my husband lying there in the dirt, covered with blood, for the rest of my days."

"Then you do have a conscience."

A hurt expression came over her. "That was harsh. I'm not entirely without morals, you know."

"Don't look to me for sympathy. You did what you did, and now you have to live with it." Fargo sighed.

"It's that way for everybody. I have things I'll take to my grave that if I could, I'd cut the memories from my brain so I never remember them again." Foremost among them was the time he came on several burning covered wagons and the remains of families bound for Oregon. One had been a baby—

"From harsh to kindly in the blink of an eye," Rose said.

Fargo turned to walk off. She just didn't understand.

Rose caught his sleeve and held him there. "I'd like to thank you another way," she whispered. "That is, if you're not that tired."

All Fargo could do was stare.

"What? We can sneak off after my girls go to sleep. They'll be all right." Rose smiled and moved her legs in an enticing manner. "What do you say, handsome?"

"I'm flattered, but no."

Rose took a step back and tilted her head. "You don't want to? I've never had a man do that."

"There's a first time for everything." Fargo smothered a yawn.

"Oh. I see. You're plumb wore out. That's all right. It's a long way to Fort Davis." Rose brushed his fingers with hers, and grinned. "My invite will stand the whole way there." She fluttered her eyelids and walked toward her youngest.

"God, I need a drink," Skye Fargo said.

16

Sissy One snuck off first and was leaning against a cottonwood, waiting. Her back was to him and she was watching a cow rub against another tree. She didn't hear him come up behind her.

Fargo grinned as he wrapped his arms around her slim waist and pulled her to him. She gasped, then giggled and glanced over her shoulder.

"So there you are, good-looking. I was beginning to think you had changed your mind."

"Not likely," Fargo said. Not after their last bout of passion. She had a fine body. Just thinking about fondling and caressing it again made him hard below his belt.

"That's one of the things I like about men," Sissy One remarked. "You don't pretend not to like it as a lot of women do."

"There are few things I like more," Fargo admitted. Cards and whiskey came closest.

"Makes two of us," Sissy One said, and went to turn to face him but he held her tight against his groin. "What are you up to?"

"As if you can't guess." Fargo kissed her neck, then ran the tip of his tongue to her earlobe and sucked on it. She cooed softly and wriggled her bottom seductively.

"Keep that up and I might get excited."

"Might?" Fargo scanned the cottonwoods to be sure they wouldn't be interrupted. He could see the spring off through the trees, and the sleeping forms of Rose and Sissy Three curled on their sides. He had made sure they were sound asleep before he slipped away.

"What are you waiting for? An invite?"

Fargo cupped both her breasts and squeezed them, hard. Again she gasped, her mouth puckering. He pinched both nipples and felt them harden to his touch.

"Ohhhh. I like it."

Fargo went on fondling and kneading them. Soon he had her moaning and grinding against him, and a bulge in his buckskins. He kissed the back of her neck and nipped her shoulder. Twisting her head, she parted her lips and rimmed them with the wet tip of her tongue. He took the hint. Their mouths met in a kiss that went on and on.

The whole while, Fargo was alert for sounds out of the ordinary—the snap of a twig, the rustle of brush, the scrape of a moccasin. The Apaches were bound to show up eventually. He figured later rather than sooner, but it never paid to take anything for granted where Apaches were involved.

Sissy One swirled her tongue. How she could taste so sweet after all they had been through, Fargo couldn't guess. But some women had that knack. Put them through hell and they came out smelling and tasting like heaven.

By now Fargo was so swollen, his pole threatened to burst his pants. It almost hurt. He ran a hand down over her flat belly to the junction of her thighs. She shivered when he slid a finger between her legs. She was as hot as the sun down there. That she didn't wear anything under the dress excited him no end. Most women wouldn't think of stepping outdoors without two or three layers of underclothes. This hill girl didn't care. She did what she liked and the rest of the world be damned. He admired that. He had some of the same trait.

"Lordy, I want you."

Fargo delved his hand up under her dress. He dallied at her thighs, savoring the smooth feel. He could run his hand over them all day. But soon he brought his fingers across soft, crinkly hair to her wet nether lips. A sharp intake of breath greeted his initial flick of a fingertip. Parting them, he rubbed, sending waves of pleasure rippling through her.

"Oh, yes!" Sissy One rose onto her bare toes, her hands on his hips, her head thrown back.

Fargo turned her so she was facing the tree, then spread her legs and pried at his belt buckle.

"What are you—?" Sissy One indulged in a delicious wicked grin. "So that's how you want it?" She braced her hands against the trunk. "Do me, handsome. Do me hard."

Hiking her dress, Fargo ran the tip of his manhood across the core of her womanhood, sparking more moans. He inserted himself an inch at a time until he was in all the way, then stood still, relishing the feel. Her inner walls contracted, a velvet sheath for his metal sword.

"Don't take all day."

It was uncommon for a woman to want to rush things. They liked a lot of touching and kissing and fondling, liked to take their time climbing to the peak. Fargo liked that too, but he was a man, and men as often as not liked get it over with and get on to other things. In this instance Fargo had added incentive: he didn't care to take an arrow in the back while his pants were down around his ankles.

Gripping her hips, Fargo commenced sliding almost out and then back in, over and over and over, slowly the first few times but then faster and faster and faster until he was pumping her like a steam engine piston and she was in the throes of sensual delight.

"Yes! Yes! Harder! Faster!"

Fargo was already thrusting into her as fast as he could. She was exquisite, this hill girl, matching him thrust for thrust, heightening his pleasure as well as hers. He could understand why Butch Jagger and Nah-tanh wanted her so much. Once they dipped their wicks into her honey pot, they couldn't get enough.

"Oh, God, oh, God, oh, God, oh, God!"

Fargo felt her gush. The same impulse came over him but he resisted. If he had to rush, fine. But another minute wouldn't hurt. It might be a spell before they could do it again, provided she was willing. With women a man never knew. One day they were in the mood, the next they'd slap any man who so much as breathed on them.

The thought brought a grin. But the grin promptly faded when Fargo realized they weren't alone. He didn't hear anything. He sensed another presence. He gazed about, thinking maybe a cow had strayed close and was watching them go to town. But it wasn't a cow.

It was Sissy Three.

Fargo froze. He was hardly ever embarrassed but he could feel his face grow warm. Unsure what to say, the best he could do was smile. Sissy Three returned it.

"Don't stop on my account."

"What was that?" Sissy One was breathing heavily, her hair over her face. "Why did you stop? I was about to spurt again." She twisted and swiped at her hair. "Oh. Damn. What the blazes are you doing there, sis?"

"I woke up and couldn't get back to sleep."

"You shouldn't have come over here."

"It was interesting. I've seen a lot of cows and horses do it only they do it slower."

"Go back to the spring."

"I've seen pigs do it, too. They do it fast, like you two. Plus they squeal an awful lot. Do you squeal much?"

Fargo said, "Not if I can help it." He started to ease out of Sissy One, but she shook her head.

"Look, little one. We'll be done in a bit. Go sit next to Ma and keep an eye skinned for Injuns."

"Can't I stay and watch the rest?"

"No. You're not half grown yet. Shoo."

"But it's fun to watch. Mr. Fargo's face looked like Pa's when he used to eat hot apple pie."

"I really need a drink," Fargo said.

"And you were sort of purple."

Fargo made a mental note to look in a mirror the next time he made love in a hotel room.

"Scat!" Sissy One said sharply. "Give us a minute or two and we'll be right there."

With a loud sigh, her little sister turned and threaded off through the cottonwoods.

"Darned brat. I'm sorry about that. She knows better than to spy on me when I'm with a fella." Sissy One shook her bottom. "Have you lost interest or are you still up for it?'

Fargo was still as hard as could be. He made sure Sissy Three wasn't looking back, and, taking hold of Sissy One's bottom, he rammed up into her as if she were a castle gate and he was a Viking battering it down. She started to cry out but caught herself and clamped her mouth shut.

Fargo didn't know why but suddenly he was at the peak. His pole was throbbing. He went on stroking her. All it would take was a nudge to send him over the precipice. Then Sissy One writhed in the throes of another orgasm, and her release triggered his.

In due course they slowed. Fargo eased out of her and stepped back to do himself up.

"That was nice. Real nice."

Fargo bent and pulled up his pants. "We can do it again provided your sister isn't around."

"Next time I'll knock her over the head with a rock first."

There were still a few hours left until they headed out. Ignoring the stares of the little one, Fargo spread out his blankets and with his saddle for a pillow he was asleep almost as soon as he laid down. A deep, dreamless sleep, that ended when someone began shaking his right shoulder. Reluctantly, he cracked his eyes open, and grunted.

"You told me to wake you when the sun was about to go down," Sissy Three said.

Fargo sat up. A welcome aroma tingled his nose. "Is that coffee I smell?"

"I took it from your saddlebags," Rose said from over by the fire she had made. "Figured we could all use some to help keep us awake tonight."

"You rummaged in my saddlebags?"

"Relax. I didn't take anything, if that's what you're worried about." Rose tapped his coffeepot with his tin cup. "It's about ready."

Sissy One was already up and on her knees at the spring, wringing her hair out.

"Usually she only washes up once a month, if that," Rose remarked. "You'd think she was going out on the town." She chuckled. "But then, I never have liked soap and water all that much myself. Lye soap makes me itch something terrible. Twice a year is good for me, and for my family, too."

That explained the dirt and the grime. But all Fargo said was, "I've met people who takes baths once a day."

"Foolishness, if you ask me. My grandma used to say that too much bathing can make a person puny."

Fargo had heard the same claim and noticed that those who said it usually needed baths the most. Rising, he stretched, then began gathering up his effects. Sissy Three helped him roll up his bedroll. "Thank you."

"I wanted to ask you a question," she said quietly.

"Ask away."

"When I grow up, do you think I should do what you and my sister were doing?"

About to hoist his saddle, Fargo paused. "That's one hell of a question, girl. Better you ask your mother."

"But that's the thing. She likes to do it, too. That's why Pa was so mad at her all the time. And Sissy One is always getting into trouble because of it. So I figured I'd ask you whether it's worth it."

Fargo hunkered. "Listen. Some things you have to decide for yourself. That's one of them. Some people don't like to do it, and that's fine for them. Some people like to do it a lot, and that's fine for them. You have to make up your mind which is best for you and then live the way you want." He mustered a grin. "So long as you're not one of those who don't like it and try to control those of us who do."

"You like it a lot, don't you?"

"I've said all I'm going to."

The girl grew thoughtful. "Why did God make us this way? Why make it so we can do that?"

"There you go again." Fargo glanced at Rose, who had found his pemmican and was making four piles. "I told you before. I'm no parson."

"I'd really like to know. You've always been nice to me. You treat me like I wish my pa had treated me. And you always tell me the truth."

"Don't make more of me than there is. But I will tell you this. I don't even know if there is a God. There are days I want to believe. Days when life is fine. Then I come on a white baby skinned alive by hostiles, or Indian women and their kids slaughtered by whites, and I want to shake my fist at the sky. What sort of God lets that happen? There are times when I think that if there is a God, God's a lunatic."

"That makes sense. Thank you. No one has ever talked to me like you do."

"You're welcome," Fargo said. Come to think of it, he had never, ever had a talk like this his whole life. The girl brought out part of him he hadn't realized was in there. He wondered if the same thing happened to parents all the time. It scared him a little.

"I guess I'll wait until I grow up to make up my mind. But I do know one thing. I won't do it as much as Ma and Sissy One do. Grandma told me once, when we were having what she called a special talk, that a girl should keep her legs crossed until a special man comes along."

"Do that, then." Fargo swung his saddle up over his back and turned to walk to the Ovaro.

"I think you're special. When I grow up, I'll find a man just like you."

"Don't," Fargo said.

"Why not?"

"A man like me will make love to you and then leave you no matter how much you don't want him to."

"You would do that?"

Fargo nodded.

Sissy Three gazed up through the cottonwoods at the darkening sky. "I wish things made more sense."

"That makes two of us," Skye Fargo said.

17

A full moon helped.

A pale glow bathed the bleak terrain, softening its harsh contours, lending the illusion they rode through a twilight realm of peaceful splendor. But the land was ugly, and brutal, and inhabited by violent men who would kill them if those men caught them.

Fargo kept that always in mind. He brought up the rear, pushing the cows as needed. Rose and Sissy Three were to one side of the cowherd. Sissy One was on the other side with the horse herd. It wouldn't do to mix the two.

Fargo rode with one hand always on his Colt. The Apaches might strike at any time, and when they did, it would be without warning. He would be lucky to get off a shot unless he heard them or saw them first, and when they wanted to be, Apaches could be ghosts.

Kill without being killed. That was the Apache creed. They had resisted the Spanish, and the Mexicans, and now the whites. They were determined to keep their land. For the whites to force them onto reservations, as had been done with so many other tribes, would take considerable doing, and cost the whites dearly.

So far the cows were behaving. They were watered and rested and as content to move as cows ever got, but by tomorrow that would change. Once the heat got to them, and there was no graze, they would become irritable and prone to spook and stampede.

Fargo wasn't looking forward to what was to come.

But he had to get the females to safety and Fort Davis was the nearest haven. If they could make it with the cows and horses, so much the better. Selling them would bring Rose and her girls hundreds of dollars. Rose had said he could have as much of it as he wanted, after all he had done for them. And he wouldn't mind a poker stake.

Now and then a coyote yipped. Once, an owl asked the eternal question of its nocturnal kind. But otherwise the night was quiet save for the tromp of hooves.

Fargo coughed. He took his hand off his Colt to loosen his red bandanna and retie the bandanna over his mouth and nose. The herd was raising a cloud of dust, the particles shimmering in the moon glow like pinpoints of silver.

Midnight came and went.

Fargo detected a slight restlessness in the cattle and wondered if they had caught the scent of a big cat. Cougars and a few jaguars roamed that country, and sometimes the smell of them sent whole herds into a panic. He was glad when they seemed to calm and plodded peacefully on.

Then Sissy Three came riding out of the dark, lashing her horse with the reins, to draw up in breathless excitement. "Ma sent me. She thinks she saw an Apache."

"She thinks?"

"Go quick. I'll stay here and do what you're doing."

Like hell, Fargo thought. Out loud he said, "No, you'll come with me." He broke from the herd and she rode at his side, her hair flying, riding as well as any girl he ever saw.

Rose had her rifle in her hands. She gave a nervous smile and pointed into the night. "Over yonder was where I saw him. Just one, shadowing us. I saw him as clear as anything."

"You're sure it was an Apache?" Fargo said.

"It could have been, yes."

"Then you didn't see him that clearly?"

"Why are you nitpicking? I saw *someone* on a horse. Who else would it be but an Apache?"

"I'll have a look." Fargo gestured to Sissy Three. "Stay with your ma. And no matter what the two of you hear, don't come after me."

"But what if you need help?" Sissy Three asked.

"Do what I tell you." Fargo gigged the Ovaro and the night closed around them. He could see for maybe forty feet; beyond that was a dark veil. He was alert for the twang of a bowstring or a stealthy tread, but he heard only the cows. He searched the ground, knowing full well it would be a fluke to spot tracks at night. But dust lay thick on the plain they were crossing, and presently he spied the clearly etched prints of a horse that had not been shod.

"Damn." Fargo had been hoping it would be another day or two before the Apaches showed. Now he and the others were in great and immediate danger.

Rose and her youngest were anxiously waiting. "Well? Was I right? Is it Apaches?"

"At least one," Fargo said.

"Where did Three Ears get the horse? We took all of theirs."

"We don't know it's him. It could be another band." Fargo gazed at the cows. "We should forget about them."

"About what? The herd?"

"We should take a few extra horses to use when ours tire and push on to the fort."

"That's a lot of money on the hoof. And it was your idea to sell them to begin with."

"You can't sell them if you're dead."

Sissy Three said, "Ma, I think we should do as he says. I don't want to die because of some stupid cows."

"That's a lot of money, daughter," Rose said again.

"Which would you rather have?" Fargo asked. "The money or your life?"

"I just hate the thought of giving them up." Rose

frowned and slapped her saddle horn. "Why can't things ever go the way they should?"

"What will it be?" Fargo prompted.

Rose muttered something, and slapped her saddle horn a second time. "All right. My girls matter more. As much as I hate the idea, we'll head for the fort."

"Good."

They swung wide behind the cow herd and over to the other side where Sissy One had the horse herd. Only when they got to where Fargo expected her to be, Sissy One, and the horse herd, were gone.

"Maybe the horses ran off and she went after them," Rose said, unable to hide her worry.

"She would have let us know." Fargo's eyes were on the dust, and the story they told.

"Maybe she fell behind for some reason," Rose refused to admit the obvious. "We should go back and look for her."

Fargo pointed. The tracks led to the west, and to his trained eyes, the new sets were a punch to his gut. "Apaches took her and the horse herd, both."

"Oh, God."

Fargo wheeled the Ovaro to bar their way, and drew rein. "I'm going after her. You two stay with the cows."

"No."

"I can ride faster alone."

"No."

"Damn it, Rose."

"Whether she is or she isn't, Sissy Three and me are going with you. We're her kin. It's ours to do."

"You're being pigheaded," Fargo said.

"And you're wasting time. She's my *daughter.* Now either come with us or get out of our way. Because you won't stop me short of shooting me."

"Please," Sissy Three said.

As best Fargo could tell, two Apaches had crept close on foot, jumped Sissy One from behind, and pulled her from her horse. One probably pinned her arms while the other clamped a hand over her mouth to keep her from shouting. Then she was thrown over an Apache mount, and all five quietly drove the horse herd off. He might have heard them only he was on the far side of the cowherd, lured there by another warrior who had deliberately let Rose see him. Typical Apache trick.

But Fargo doubted that the Apaches expected him to find out so soon. They must have figured the cowherd would move on and it would be hours before anyone discovered Sissy One and the horse herd were missing.

Fargo rode as fast as he dared. After a mile he slowed, much to Rose's annoyance. "We don't want them to hear us coming if we can help it," he explained. But she wasn't mollified.

It was rare for Apaches to be careless, but these were. An orange and red dot was Fargo's first inkling that maybe, just maybe, he would be able to save Sissy One. Drawing rein, he said, "See that?"

"It's them!" Rose exclaimed.

"This time I am going on alone, on foot. No matter what you hear, stay put." Fargo had his reason for saying that.

"No."

"Not again, damn it."

"You know as well as I do why they've stopped."

Sissy Three asked, "Why, Ma?"

"Never you mind." Rose didn't take her eyes off Fargo. "If we hurry, we might be able to stop them."

"If we hurry, they'll hear us," Fargo argued. "These are Apaches we're talking about."

"All the more reason for us not to sit here." Rose swung down. "Are you coming or not?"

"And what about your youngest? Do we leave her here all alone?"

"She comes with us." Rose beckoned to Sissy Three. "Hustle, girl. Your sister needs us."

Since Fargo couldn't stop them, he led the way. The dot became a flame and the flame became a small fire. The last hundred yards Fargo traveled on his belly.

There were six warriors, and all were young. Not one had seen twenty winters. Older warriors wouldn't have stopped. Older warriors would have gone on to wherever their people were camped and shown off the spoils of their raid. But these six had something else on their minds.

Fargo wished to God that Rose and Sissy Three hadn't come along. The girl in particular. To see her older sister staked out like that. To see what the Apaches were doing. As yet, though, they hadn't. They were behind him, and a boulder blocked their view. Quickly turning, he whispered, "This is as far as you go."

"Don't you ever learn?" Rose tried to crawl around him but he shifted to prevent her. "Get out of my way."

"For once will you listen? Keep Sissy Three here. I'll tend to this."

Rose regarded him with suspicion. "What don't you want us to see?" Before Fargo could stop her, she rose onto her knees. Stiffening, she raised a hand to her mouth. Then, lunging upright, she ran toward the fire.

"Stay here!" Fargo commanded Sissy Three, and, whirling, he raced after her mother.

Fortunately, the Apaches were so engrossed in what they were doing, all of them talking and several laughing when blood splattered the one doing the carving, that they didn't hear Rose Sands until she was almost on top of them. She shot the first one to turn toward her smack in the throat. She shot the second in the head. Another rushed her as the last three scattered. His knife was out and held high, and he was on the verge of burying it in her chest when Fargo stroked the Henry's trigger.

Rose stood over her eldest and bowed her head. "Dear Lord, no. Not another one."

Fargo could barely stand to look. The skinless flesh, the blood, the mouth without lips and the missing nose—

it churned his stomach. Bile rose in his throat but he swallowed it back down. Remembering the Apaches, he turned.

Hooves drummed, growing rapidly fainter.

"I think they're gone," Fargo said, and turned back again. Rose was on her knees, clasping Sissy One's hand. And not six feet away, there was Sissy Three, as pale as the moonlight, her eyes as wide as saucers.

"How could they do that, Ma? How could anyone do that?"

"They're not human." Rose raised her eldest's fingers to her lips and kissed them. "Now I've lost two of my girls."

Sissy One wasn't dead yet. The sticks in her eyes, her intestines spilled over her hip—but she wasn't dead. Her mouth moved and blood trickled out. "Ma?" she gurgled. "Is that you?"

Rose nodded, and then said, her voice thick with emotion, "It's me, sweet one. Lie still."

"They did terrible things to me."

"I can see—" Rose said, and couldn't say more.

"I hurt, Ma. I hurt so much. Make it stop, Ma. Do what you have to and make the hurting stop."

Sissy Three started to cry.

Rose sniffled and looked up at Fargo. "I can't. God help me, I gave birth to her and I can't."

Fargo couldn't blame her. But he didn't expect what she said next, and it shocked him.

"You have to."

"Not that," Fargo said. "Anything but that." It would be another of those memories he wanted to forget but never could.

"There's no one else. You must have some feeling for her, after carrying on with her like you've done."

Fargo felt like cursing the heavens.

"Please." Rose held out a blood-speckled hand in appeal. "She could last half a day or more. Think of how she'll suffer."

Fargo's whole body was tingling and his mouth had gone dry. "Get your youngest out of here."

"I'll watch," Sissy Three said.

"Like hell, you will."

Rose intervened, saying, "She's old enough. Let her stay. I don't want her to ever forget."

"You want her to remember *this*?" Fargo gestured.

"She'll remember, and she won't let herself be caught like Sissy One did. Please, Skye. I'm begging you."

Fargo felt completely and utterly drained.

"Spare my firstborn. Do it. Do it now."

18

They each took an extra horse, leading it by a rope. Fargo was tempted to take two or three but the mother and the girl were in a state of shock and could barely handle the one. Twice Rose slowed, tears flowing, and he had to urge her to hasten on.

The young warriors who got away might be following them. Three Ears might be after them. Then there was Earl Jagger, if he was still alive, out there somewhere and filled with hate for the Sandses.

Fargo told himself that Rose and her littlest one weren't going to share the fate of the rest of their family. Everything would be fine once they reached Fort Davis. He tried not to dwell on the fact that it would take days to get there, across drought-stricken land with enemies everywhere.

Fargo hated leaving the cows but they moved too slow. Rose and Sissy Three could use the money their sale would bring. Most would perish, dying a hideous death from thirst and starvation, unless the Apaches got hold of them. Then they would be eaten, or driven into Mexico and sold.

Fargo shook off a yawn. He was tired, bone tired, and worn. And not just his body. What he had to do to Sissy One would stick with him the rest of his days. He would try to shut it out, but it would come to him in the sleepless hours of the night or when he least wanted it to, and he would remember every vivid detail, and wither inside.

Life in the wild was vicious. There was no other word

to describe it. Nature was not just a harsh mistress; she was a cruel one, with no mercy for the unwary. The elements, the hard land, the savage beasts and men, made for constant perils, and woe to whoever was careless.

A faint brightening of the eastern sky heralded the new dawn. Fargo cast about for a place to lie low and found a gully that would provide shade most of the day. There was no water to be had but they had been riding only one night and their mounts, while weary, would make it through another.

Rose and Sissy Three did not say a word. They curled up side by side; the mother's arm over her daughter, closed their eyes, and were soon tossing and turning in fitful sleep.

Fargo stayed up a while. He went to the mouth of the gully, climbed to the rim, and watched their back trail. He didn't see anyone. He didn't spot dust tendrils. For the time being they were safe.

Lying on his back with his head in his hands, Fargo waited for sleep to claim him. He needed rest, needed it badly, but his mind refused to shut down. He thought about all that had happened since he stumbled on the Sands family, and about how sometimes a man might do what he thought best only to make things worse.

Life could be so damn fickle.

That was his last thought before drifting off. At first the slightest noises woke him, but then he was in a deep sleep from which he didn't rouse until the sun was sinking in the west. He rolled over, not ready to get up yet, and blinked in surprise.

Rose and Sissy Three were gone.

Fargo sat up. They weren't anywhere nearby. Their horses were still there so he figured they had gone for a walk. But after a while he grew concerned, and rising, he moved down the gully. But he found no trace of them. The ground was too hard to show footprints.

"Damn it."

The shadows were lengthening. Twilight would soon fall. Fargo hoped to God they hadn't wandered off and gotten lost. Finding them in that maze of rock and dirt would take some doing.

Then the Ovaro nickered, and Fargo hurried back up the gully to find the two he was worried about hunkered near the horses, talking. "Where have you two been?"

Rose pointed up the gully. "We have something to show you."

"What?"

"Come see for yourself."

Sissy Three's hand slipped into his as they climbed. The gully opened onto a shelf that overlooked the country to the east. A mile away or so, smoke curled into the sky.

"Apaches, you think?" Rose asked him.

Fargo doubted it. "Too much smoke for Indians." They had more sense than to advertise their presence.

"Whites, then?" Rose said excitedly. "Maybe it's an army patrol. We should go find out."

Fargo agreed. They saddled up and were soon under way. Rose rode to the right of him, Sissy Three to the left. He would rather they rode in single file but they seemed to take comfort from being close to him so he let them.

"The worst is over. I feel it in my bones," Rose said confidently. "A month from now Texas will be a bitter memory."

"We never should have come," Sissy Three said softly.

Rose smiled serenely. "I can't wait to see the green hills of Georgia again. To smell the magnolias and the lilacs. To hear the crickets at night and watch the fireflies. To sip a mint julep and feel the cool evening breeze and listen to the bullfrogs croak."

"I bet you miss it, too," Fargo said to the girl.

"I missed my cousins and my friends for a while. Now

I miss my pa and my sisters. I miss them a terrible lot." Sissy Three paused. "I can't stop thinking about them. About how they died."

Rose said, "It's best not to dwell on it, daughter. Force yourself to think about other things. Pleasant things. Happy things."

"I've tried and I can't."

"Give yourself time. They say it heals all wounds. A year from now you won't hardly give your pa any thought at all."

"How can you say that, Ma? I thought you said you loved him."

"Don't ever think different. But you can't do as some women do and let love blind you to life. You have to be practical. Now that your pa is gone, I'll find me another man. I'm fairly young yet. I still have my looks."

"Oh, Ma."

"What? Ask Fargo, here, if you don't believe me. He's never gotten cow eyed over a woman in his life, I'd bet. And I'll be switched if I'll spend the rest of mine moping and pining after Cletus when I have a lot of good years left."

"I don't understand you sometimes, Ma. I truly don't."

"It's simple. I live for the moment. The good moments. The bad moments I can do without. You'd do well to do the same. We're none of us long in this world, and we do well to make the most of it."

Fargo shared some of her sentiments. He always took each day as it came, exactly as she did. But he would never do as she had done; marry someone, then carry on with every Tom, Dick and Harry who came down the pike, and drive the man she married to drink and violent fits.

"There has to be more to life," Sissy Three said. "There has to."

"What do you know, young as you are?" Rose responded. "Some folks say there is, but where's the proof? We are who we are and we do what we do, and that's that."

Fargo slowed. They were close enough to smell the smoke. It rose from behind a bluff. "I'll go see who it is."

"You should know better by now."

Stars winked and twinkled, and somewhere a coyote yipped.

At the base of the bluff Fargo drew rein. Alighting, he palmed his Colt. "On foot from here."

Fortunately, they didn't lack for cover. Soon they were near enough for Fargo to see the fire and those who had made it.

"I'll be!" Rose whispered. "They got away from the Apaches."

It was Earl Jagger, his son Butch, and their two hands, Reese and Vern. They looked as if they had been through hell. Vern's shoulder was crudely bandaged, the bandage caked with dry blood. They had no coffee and nothing to eat and were staring morosely into the flames. Close by, next to a small stone tank of water under an outcropping surrounded by brush, stood a pair of exhausted Indian ponies. Evidently, the four men had been riding double.

Fargo wanted nothing to do with them and turned. "Back the way we came," he said.

"I want to talk to Earl."

"The last time you saw him, you were trying to kill each other," Fargo reminded her.

"I don't care." Rose stood and marched off, Sissy Three following suit. "Stay here if you want."

Fargo bit off an oath. Short of clubbing her over the head and throwing her over his shoulder, he had no recourse but to go along. Thumbing back the Colt's hammer, he caught up. "Has anyone ever told you that you are a pain in the ass?"

"Just about everybody," Rose said with mock sweetness. Then she stopped and raised her voice. "Hello the camp! Earl Jagger! I'd like to come in if you give me your word you won't shoot."

All four jumped to their feet. Earl and his son leveled rifles. Reese's twin revolvers streaked from their holsters. Vern put his hand on his six-gun but didn't draw it.

"Who's that?" Earl Jagger hollered. "Who's there?"

"Don't your ears work? It's me. Rose Sands. I have my youngest with me, and Fargo is along. Do we have your word or not?"

Earl said something to the others then replied, "We won't shoot! But keep your hands where we can see them and don't try any tricks. I don't trust you, woman."

Rose laughed. Holding her rifle by the barrel, she extended her arms and advanced. "Here we come! Watch those trigger fingers."

Sissy Three did the same, only she was so small, and her rifle so heavy, the stock dragged on the ground.

Fargo stayed a few steps behind them and to one side, the Colt close to his leg.

The moment Rose entered the circle of firelight, Earl Jagger barked, "That's close enough! What are you doing here?"

"I could ask you the same thing," Rose said amiably. "The last we saw, the Apaches were after you."

Butch Jagger said, "They almost had us, too. They were closing in when suddenly they lit out and left us. But not before Vern took an arrow."

"Strange them doing that," Vern remarked.

It wasn't strange to Fargo. The Apaches had rushed back to try to stop the Sandses and him from running their horses off.

"We found these two critters and decided to head for Fort Davis," Butch had gone on with a jerk of his thumb at the Indian mounts.

"We're heading there, too," Sissy Three said.

Earl was peering into the dark. "Where's that husband of yours? And your other two girls?"

"Dead," Rose said.

Butch appeared stricken. "All of them? Sissy One, too?"

"Afraid so," Rose confirmed. "The Apaches got hold of her. There wasn't anything we could do but put her out of her misery."

The Jaggers lowered their rifles but Reese still had his Smith and Wessons trained on them.

"Say the word, boss, and I'll buck them out in gore."

"Sheath your horns," Earl told him. "We're past that now." He beckoned. "Come join us. I give you my range word we won't harm you."

"You're not mad about your cows and the hands you lost?"

"Of course I am," Earl admitted. "But I also want to go on breathing, and I have a proposition to make."

Rose indicated Reese. "I don't trust him. Have him holster his hardware and I'll hear you out."

"You heard her," Earl said.

Unable to hide his anger, Reese twirled the Smith and Wessons into their holsters but kept his hands on them. "You're making a mistake, big sugar. She'll shoot us as soon as we turn our backs."

"Then don't turn around," Earl said. Again he beckoned. "Please. Hear me out, Rose. It's to both our benefit."

Fargo took a few steps to the right so he could cover them better. Vern gave him a wan smile. Reese scowled.

"I can't believe Sissy One is gone," Butch said forlornly. "I was fixing to ask her to marry me." He moved aside so Rose and her youngest could stand by the fire if they wanted. "She was beautiful, that oldest of yours."

"My middle girl was a peach, too," Rose said quietly. "I've lost too many dear to me."

"I've lost good men," Earl Jagger said. "And I don't care to lose my son or my own life. So here's my notion. We join forces, the two of us. We bury the hatchet, call a truce, and make for the fort together."

"There *is* strength in numbers," Rose agreed.

Earl Jagger nodded. "Fetch your horses and you can spend the night with us. At first light we'll head out."

Fargo had a troubling thought. What if all the rancher wanted were their mounts? Those Apache horses wouldn't last another day. He tried to catch Rose's eye to warn her but she was staring across the fire at Reese.

"What do you say?" Earl asked.

"I'm inclined to accept," Rose told him. "But we've been riding at night and resting during the day. The scout, here, thinks it's safer that way, and I agree."

"So you want us to head out now? Is that it?" Earl scratched the stubble on his chin. "I don't know. We've been pushing hard all day and we're about wore out."

Rose cradled her rifle, and shrugged. "It's up to you. But we'll be that much closer to Fort Davis when we stop tomorrow night."

"I'm for it, Pa," Butch said.

"Me, too," Vern said.

Reese was still scowling. "I don't trust her, boss. She's tricky, this Southern bitch. I think she's up to something."

"That I am," Rose said, and shot him.

19

It happened so fast there was nothing anyone could do to stop her. Rose simply swung the muzzle of her rifle at Reese's face and blew a hole the size of a walnut in his forehead. She already had the rifle cocked; all she had to do was squeeze the trigger.

Butch Jagger and Vern both jumped. Earl Jagger took a half step toward Rose, glanced at Reese oozing to the ground and the blood and brains oozing from the hole, and swore.

Sissy Three had the strangest reaction: she smiled.

Or maybe it wasn't so strange, Fargo reflected. Reese had shot Sissy Two. To Sissy Three, he was getting his due.

Butch Jagger showed the whites of his eyes. "What in God's name did you do that for?"

"Relax, boy. I'm not out to shoot anyone else. But this one"—Rose nodded at Reese—"killed one of my girls." She shifted so her rifle was pointed at Earl Jagger. "Do you hold it against me? Or is the truce still on?"

"Bitch," Earl said.

"That's beside the point. Do you still want to join forces, as you put it? Or should we go to war?"

"You're the most contrary female I've ever met," the rancher told her. "And that takes some doing."

"You flatter me," Rose replied.

"And you're as loco as they come."

"I have my faults, the same as most any person. I've always been too fond of men, and could never be true to my husband even though—I swear on my mother's grave—I loved him. But you have your flaws, too. You take what you don't have the right to take. You kill children—"

"Damn it, she was firing at us!" Earl exploded. "All of you were! What were we to do?" He nodded at Reese. "He was shooting into the dark when we escaped from your cabin. I doubt he even knew he killed her."

"Don't give me that. There was plenty of light from the fire. And even if he didn't see her, he shot at her rifle flashes, which is the same thing." Rose chuckled. "Ironic, isn't it? I killed him because he was a good shot."

"Like I said," Earl responded, "you're one crazy bitch."

"No more name calling," Rose warned. "Or our friendship comes to an end and only one of us rides away from here."

Earl balled his fists, then visibly relaxed and held his hands out to her, palms up. "All right. I'll honor our truce. But only until we get to Fort Davis."

"Fair enough," Rose said.

Vern had rolled Reese over. "What about the body, Mr. Jagger? We don't have anything to bury him with."

"We can't be bothered with Apaches skulking about. Drag it off and leave it for the coyotes and the buzzards."

"It doesn't seem right."

"Fine. Then you dig a grave with your good arm, and if you take an arrow in the back or your throat is slit, don't holler for help because you'll have asked for it."

Butch bent over the body. "I'll help you drag him off, Vern."

"I'm obliged."

Earl Jagger looked at Fargo. "And what about you, mister? You haven't said a word since you showed up."

"I'm shy," Fargo said.

"Like hell you are."

"Let's have some coffee and then we'll head out," Rose proposed. "Fargo has some in his saddlebags." She sat with Sissy Three in her lap, both with their rifles across their legs.

Fargo deemed it safe to fetch their horses, and when he came back, Butch and Vern had returned and were across the fire, next to Earl. Vern offered to make the coffee and Fargo sat between the two camps, as it were, his Colt in his hand.

Earl Jagger looked from him to Rose and back again. "This is a hell of a note. No one trusts anyone."

"Whose fault is that?" Rose asked. "You're the one who came on our land and took over our spring."

"Don't start."

Butch cleared his throat. "We're in a tight. It wouldn't surprise me any if the Apaches know right where we are. They'll guess we're heading for the fort and try to stop us."

"By 'stop' you mean kill," Vern said, "and I'm powerful fond of breathing."

"No stinking Apache is going to kill me," Earl Jagger declared.

"Why is that?" Rose asked. "Do arrows bounce off that thick hide of yours?"

"If I know Apaches," Vern said, "they'll hit us when we least expect. It will come out of the blue, and half of us will be dead before we can bat an eye."

"That's looking at the bright side," Earl told him.

Fargo agreed with the cowhand. All the more reason for them to focus on staying alive and to quit their bickering.

Presently the coffee was ready. Rose took a loud sip and grinned at Vern. "Right fine. You've had a lot of practice."

"That I have, ma'am," the cowboy said.

Fargo poured a cup for himself, downed the coffee in several quick gulps, and poured another.

"Don't hog it, mister," Earl Jagger said.

"There's enough for all of us, Pa," Butch told him. "We'll need it to stay awake."

"If it were up to me, we'd wait until dawn."

Rose snickered. "Stay here if you want. But Fargo and my girl and me are lighting a shuck. You'd be smart to do the same."

"I agree, ma'am," Vern said.

"You would," Earl snapped.

Fargo kept one eye on the horses. The animals would smell or hear Apaches before they did. But they showed no alarm.

"Tell me something, Earl," Rose said. "What brought a cantankerous cuss like you to these remote parts?"

"What do you care?"

"I'm curious, is all."

"It's simple. I don't care much for people."

"Now there's a shock."

"Spare me your tart tongue. I used to live in east Texas but it got overrun with people. Used to be, a man could ride for days without seeing another living soul, but now there are more homesteaders and squatters than you can shake a stick at."

Fargo saw the Ovaro raise its head and stare to the north. Without being obvious, he slowly twisted so he could see behind him. The dark hid whatever, or whoever, was out there.

"I figured to be the first in these parts," the rancher had gone on. "I laid claim to ten times as many acres as I had before, and reckoned on spending the rest of my days here. Then along came the damn drought. And the Apaches began to act up."

"Life is one kick in the teeth after another," Rose said.

The Ovaro pricked its ears and raised its head even higher.

Easing into a crouch, Fargo reached for the coffee pot. "How fast can all of you get on your horses?"

"Vern and me are riding double," Butch said. "So not fast at all. Why do you ask?"

"It could be we have company."

"Red company?" Earl Jagger said.

Butch gazed around, puzzled. "Where? I don't see anyone. Maybe you're mistaken."

An arrow proved Fargo right. It whizzed out of the night and pierced Vern's chest with a loud *thwuck*. Butch leaped up and fired in the direction the arrow came from, shouting needlessly, "Injuns!"

Everyone else scurried for their mounts. Fargo took precious seconds to bend over the fallen cowboy, who, amazingly, grinned.

"This has been a hell of a week," he said, and died.

Whirling, Fargo sprang to the Ovaro. Rose and Sissy Three were already mounted. So was Earl Jagger. Butch had hold of the other Apache horse but it was spooked by the commotion and shying away from him.

"Stand still, damn you!"

Two more arrows followed the first. One missed Earl as he bent low and used his spurs. The other streaked down out of the ether and would have transfixed Fargo except that he swung onto the Ovaro and the shaft cleaved the space where he had been standing.

"Ride!"

Everyone fled. Everyone but Butch, who couldn't get the spooked horse to obey. And Fargo, who reined over, snagged the rope bridle the Apaches favored, and held the animal still while Butch hastily climbed on.

War whoops shattered the night and a pack of swarthy figures bounded toward them.

Fargo turned in the saddle and fired two swift shots. Then Butch was on his horse and together they raced after the others. A few more arrows sought them but missed. Several rifles cracked, and leaden wasps buzzed their ears.

Fargo hugged his saddle. He glanced back, saw Vern's prone form, and frowned. He liked that cowboy. Then he had to knuckle down to riding. In broken country, in the dark, it was always dangerous.

Butch was behind him, saying, "Not Vern! Not Vern! Not Vern! Not Vern!"

Fargo hadn't seen Three Ears but that didn't mean the wily warrior wasn't with their attackers. He hadn't seen horses, either, but that could be because the Apaches snuck up on foot. Either way, the band would be after them. And the shots, carrying far, would alert any other Apaches in the area.

Another minute of pounding flight resulted in Fargo spying figures ahead. He tensed, but it was Rose and Sissy Three. They had stopped to wait for him. He drew rein in a swirl of dust and glanced back. No Apaches. "Are both of you all right?"

"I was scared," Sissy Three said.

"Where's my pa?" Butch asked.

Rose pointed to the south. "Hell bent for leather. When it comes to Apaches, he spooks easy, doesn't he?"

"My pa ain't yellow, if that's what you're saying."

"Keep riding," Fargo said.

More pounding of hooves, more dust in their nose and in their mouth. Never knowing when an arrow or a bullet would claim them. But nothing happened and after an hour Fargo drew rein to rest their horses. Sissy Three needed rest, too; she looked terribly tired.

Butch Jagger was a bundle of worry. "Where could my pa have got to? Why haven't we caught up to him?"

"He probably won't stop until he reaches Fort Davis," Rose teased.

"My pa's no coward," Butch declared. "I reckon he was right about you. Your oldest daughter was a daisy but you are a prickly cactus."

"Oh, hell, boy. Where's your sense of humor?"

Butch responded, "I haven't had anything to laugh about since this damn drought began. And now that Sissy One is gone, I may never laugh again."

Rose sobered and cocked her head. "You loved her, for real and for true, didn't you?"

"More than anything. She was the friendliest, nicest, sweetest girl I ever met."

Fargo almost said, *I'll bet.*

"She was easy to care for," Butch said. "I would have been proud to be her husband."

"She wasn't looking for one," Rose said, "but I thank you, just the same. I loved her, too, boy."

"Quit calling me that. I'm a grown man, in case you haven't noticed."

Rose chuckled. "Just because a male fills out a man's britches doesn't always make him a man."

"That makes no kind of sense."

"All I'm saying—"

Fargo held up a hand and she stopped. He thought he had heard a sound.

He turned, his saddle creaking, and strained his ears, but nothing. "I guess it's all right."

"Do you still aim to ride until dawn?" Butch asked.

"Would you rather have Apaches breathing down your neck?" Fargo rejoined.

"I'm beat, is all. We rode all day and now here I am, riding all night. I don't mind admitting I'm plumb wore out."

"Hang in there," Rose said. "I'm starting to take a shine to you."

"Ma," Sissy Three said.

"Let's go." Fargo tapped his spurs and held to a walk.

Sissy Three rode alongside him and glanced at him several times before she asked what was on her mind.

"We won't make it, will we?"

"We will if I can help it."

"I want you to know," she said, and stopped.

"Know what?"

"I thank you for all you've done for us. I almost wish I was as old as Sissy One so I could repay you."

"I won't let anything happen to you," Skye Fargo vowed.

"Don't make a promise you can't keep," Sissy Three said. "I've learned the truth about life. I know the secret."

"What might that be?"

"That the only reason we're born is to die, and there's not a blessed thing we can do about it."

"You are learning," Fargo said.

20

On through the night they rode. On through the dark and the ever-present danger, never knowing from one minute to the next if the Apaches would strike. They rode and they worried.

Fargo stopped often to spare their horses. The Ovaro was holding up well. So were Rose's and her daughter's mounts. But they had rested all day. Butch Jagger's horse was showing signs of playing out, and twice now Butch had hollered for Fargo to stop sooner than Fargo intended. This last time, Butch's mount hung its head, its sides heaving.

"This sorrel won't go much farther," Butch mentioned the obvious. "Either we make camp or I'll have to ride double with one of you."

"It won't be with me or my girl," Rose said.

Fargo didn't want Butch riding double with him, either. But they couldn't just strand him there. He gazed at the starry sky. Another couple of hours and dawn would break. "We're out in the open here. Let's find a better spot."

A ravine held promise. Its steep sides hid them and would give needed shade during the worst of the heat. Fargo didn't like that there was only one way in or out but it would have to do. He went to strip the Ovaro and thought better of it. "Leave your saddles on," he said to Rose and Sissy Three.

"How come? Do you know something we don't?"

"We might have to fan the breeze in a hurry." Fargo

had a feeling—call it intuition—and he'd learned to trust his feelings.

"It's strange we haven't seen any sign of my pa," Butch mentioned. "He wouldn't go off and leave me."

Fargo wasn't so sure but he kept it to himself. They hunkered down and he untied his bedroll and spread out his blanket for the Sandses, saying, "I'll keep watch a while. You two turn in."

"I'm awful hungry, Ma," Sissy Three said.

Fargo shared the last of his pemmican, keeping a few pieces for himself. Chewing slowly so they would last longer, he took the Henry and moved to the ravine mouth. He climbed the steep side as high as he could go, dug in his heels, and waited.

From his roost Fargo could see Rose and Sissy Three curled up on his blanket, and Butch on his back. He would like to join them but first he must make sure it was safe.

Sunrise was spectacular. A shade of pink splashed the horizon, changing to bright orange and red as the aerial furnace climbed into the vault of sky. Blue replaced the black, and the stars faded.

The short plain they had crossed was empty of life. But it didn't stay empty. Shimmering in the rising heat haze, a stick figure appeared. Then another, and a third, until Fargo counted seven, all told. They were on foot, loping with the easy, tireless, gait of wolves.

Fargo reckoned it would be twenty minutes yet before they got there. Dirt and dust cascaded from under his boots, he quickly descended and ran up the ravine. The three of them were sleeping. He shook Rose until she mumbled and stirred and opened her eyes.

"It's afternoon already? Why do I feel like I've only been asleep a short while?"

"Because you have. Get up. You and your youngest are going on without me." Fargo turned to wake Butch.

"Hold on. It's the Apaches, isn't it?"

"Smack on our trail. I'll hold them here as long as I can. It will buy you the time you need."

Rose sat up. "After all you've done for us, do you really expect me to tuck tail and run?"

"I'm thinking of her," Fargo said, with a nod at Sissy Three. "She's the last one you have left."

"Don't remind me, damn you."

"You'll have no daughters at all if those Apaches get their hands on her. For once don't argue. Save her, and whatever happens to me will be worth it."

Rose grabbed hold of his wrist. "I wouldn't do this if you weren't making me. I want you know that."

Their eyes locked, and Fargo said in genuine admiration. "Like you said, you have your flaws but you're no coward."

"Thank you for that."

Butch refused to wake up. He muttered and swatted at Fargo's hand and finally Fargo stepped back and kicked him in the side.

Howling in pain, the younger Jagger came up off the ground with his hand on his six-shooter. "What the hell?"

"Apaches," Fargo said simply. "You're leaving with the ladies."

"Wait. You can't take them by your lonesome. I should stay and help," Butch gazed down the ravine. "How many are there, anyhow?"

"I didn't count them," Fargo lied. "Hurry. There's not much time."

They walked the horses out so as not to raise dust, and once around the ravine, climbed on.

Rose looked at him. "I hate running out on you."

Sissy Three had tears in her eyes.

"Take care of your mother," Fargo said.

Butch Jagger asked, "Are you sure you don't want me to stay?"

Fargo shook his head. Jagger would only get himself

killed. "Get these ladies to the fort. I'll be there in a couple of days if all goes well."

"Skye—" Rose began.

Fargo held up a hand. "None of that." He smiled, and smacked their animals, and didn't linger to watch them ride off. Jogging back into the ravine, he climbed to his vantage point. The Apaches were less than a hundred yards out, spread in a skirmish line. A warrior was on one knee, examining the ground.

It was Three Ears.

Fargo raised the Henry. Something, maybe the gleam of sunlight off the barrel or the brass receiver, caused one of the Apaches to yell a warning, and in the blink of an eye they scattered. Fargo fixed a bead on Three Ears but the earth seemed to swallow him.

Switching the sights to another, Fargo fired, the boom of the Henry loud in the ravine's confines. Out on the plain his target clutched at his chest, took one more stride, and collapsed.

Six to one, Fargo told himself, and levered another round into the Henry's chamber. But they had melted away, the six, as if they had never been there. Common sense goaded Fargo to get the hell out of there while he still could but he had promised to buy Sissy Three and the others time, and buy them that time he would.

Now came the cat and mouse.

Fargo had the advantage. The Apaches couldn't get at him unless they entered the ravine, and there they would be easy targets. He probed every bush, every boulder, every patch of earth that did not seem natural. But it was as if the red specters had turned invisible. Even knowing they were there he couldn't spot them. It was frustrating as hell.

The Apaches would take their time. They would bottle him in, and only then would they attack. Apaches were nothing if not thorough.

Then a bush moved.

Fargo sighted on the center, and fired. The screech

that greeted his shot was the only proof he scored; the Apache never showed. Sliding a few feet lower, he pressed close to the side to make it harder for them to spot him.

The sun climbed. The masters of stealth never showed themselves.

Fargo tried not to let his mind drift, but he was only human. He thought of his travels, of the people he had met, the women he had held in his arms, the whiskey and the cards. Some would say he had squandered his life. But all in all, he had few regrets.

A boulder's shadow was longer than it should be.

Wedging the Henry to his shoulder, Fargo aimed carefully. It wouldn't be fatal but it would slow them some. He held his breath to steady his arms, waited a second, and stroked the trigger. This time the Apache leaped up, blood spurting from a shattered knee, and staggered toward a bigger boulder. Quickly, Fargo worked the Henry's lever. As he did two rifles cracked and lead smacked on either side of him. He fixed a bead on the Apache's head, just below the ear, and fired. Without a sound, the warrior folded, twitched a bit, and was still.

Angry cries and howls filled the air.

Fargo slid lower down. A ridge of dirt, a mound really, offered temporary haven. He rolled onto his back and let out a long breath. So far, so good, but he had been lucky he hadn't taken a slug and it went without saying luck was as fragile as an eggshell.

"You hear my words, white-eye?"

To say Fargo was surprised was an understatement. Rolling onto his side, he removed his hat and peered over the mound. "I hear you, Three Ears."

"You shoot two Shis-Inday."

"Thanks for letting me know," Fargo taunted. So the odds were really five to one.

"We kill you slow, white-eye. You take long time die."

"Come and get me," Fargo challenged. "Here I am."

But where were they? He could hear Three Ears as clear as anything and thought he had an idea where Three Ears must be hiding but he couldn't see him.

"You white-eye friend of Cat Woman. Three Ears remember you."

"Cat Woman?" Fargo repeated. "Is that what your people call Rose Sands?"

"She claw her man like cat. She hiss and scratch. She fight, that one."

Fargo reasoned that so long as he kept Three Ears talking, the Apaches wouldn't attack. "You sound like you admire her."

"Three Ears like Cat Woman. She proud, like Apache."

"If you like her so much, why did your people kill her husband and her oldest girl?"

"Sissy One go to other side?"

"They tortured her. Cut her to pieces," Fargo related. "So much for your friendship."

"Three Ears not kill, white-eye. Other Shis-Inday must do."

"Another band? I figured as much." Fargo kept trying to spot him, and couldn't. "Tell you what. Why don't you go your way and I'll go mine and no one else has to die."

Three Ears uttered a half bark, half laugh. "You funny, white-eye. You kill us. We kill you."

"I'm still here," Fargo said. And then it hit him. Apaches *never* did what Three Ears was doing. They *never* talked to an enemy. Apaches were also *devious*, and never did anything without a reason. And what reason could Three Ears have for doing what no other Apache ever did? Whipping around, Fargo turned toward the top of the ravine. He was a shade too late.

Their ploy had worked. While Three Ears kept Fargo talking, two warriors had climbed to the top of the ravine, and as Fargo turned, they leaped. In the split second before they slammed into him, Fargo recognized one of them as Nah-tanh. And then Fargo was smashed onto his back so hard, he felt for sure his spine had shattered. Limbs pinwheeling, he slid toward the bottom.

Nah-tanh and the other Apache yipped and came after him, leaping like mountain goats.

Fargo had lost the Henry. He clawed at his Colt and cleared leather just as he came to an abrupt stop in a swirl of dust. The one Apache was almost on top of him, a knife poised to stab. Flat on his back, Fargo fanned the Colt. Once, twice, and the Apache twisted and stumbled but didn't go down. Fargo fanned a third shot and the Apache's left eye burst in a spray of gore.

Instantly, Fargo sought to scramble to his feet but Nah-tanh reached him and a moccasin-clad foot caught him flush in the ribs. Fargo's body exploded with agony. His vision blurred. But only for a moment. It cleared as a foot arced at his face. Catching hold of Nah-tanh's ankle, Fargo wrenched with all his strength.

Nah-tanh crashed down. Pain never stopped an Apache, though, and he was up in a crouch in the bat of an eye, his blade low in front of him.

Fargo leveled the Colt, or tried to. A blow to his wrist sent the revolver flying. The knife lanced at him and he grabbed Nah-tanh's arm. Locked together, they grappled, Nah-tanh's face contorted in fury, Fargo keenly aware that the rest of the Apaches would come on the run and unless he ended the fight and ended it quickly, he would die as Sissy One had died, mutilated and suffering.

Fargo drove his knee into Nah-tanh's chest, into his hip. But the tip of the knife inched nearer to his throat. Another few seconds and it would be over. So Fargo did the only thing he could think of: he slammed his forehead against Nah-tanh's nose. Cartilage crunched and scarlet spewed.

Nah-tanh drove his shoulder against Fargo's chest, knocking him back. The knife thudded to the dirt. Fargo threw an uppercut that caught the young warrior hard on the jaw and rocked him. But the next moment Nah-tanh had scooped up his fallen blade.

Fargo hurled himself to one side. A stinging sensation shot up his arm; the knife had drawn blood but the cut wasn't deep. He spied his Colt, and pounced. Thumbing back the hammer as he spun, he shot Nah-tanh in the chest and when Nah-tanh barely slowed, shot him in the throat.

The Colt was empty.

With Nah-tanh thrashing and gurgling at his feet, Fargo began reloading. Apaches filled the ravine mouth and flew toward him. He had only three cartridges in the cylinder, but it had to do. He fired and a warrior dropped and fired again and a second warrior pitched headfirst and then the last Apache reached him, and the last Apache was Three Ears.

A rifle barrel caught Fargo across the head. He went down, pulsing with torment. He tried to bring up his Colt.

"You die now, white-eye," Three Ears said, and put the muzzle of his rifle to Fargo's cheek.

There was a shot, just one. The front of Three Ears's chest exploded outward. Eyes wide, he teetered, turning toward the mouth of the ravine and the person who had shot him. "Not girl!" he blurted, and died.

Smoke curled from Sissy Three's rifle. "I couldn't leave you," she said. "I just had to come back."

Hooves hammered. Rose drew rein and vaulted down to scoop her youngest into her arms. "I told you to stay with me! What if you had been killed?"

Sissy Three was looking at Fargo. "I had to help my friend."

Fargo slowly stood. The worst was over. Now all he had to do was get them to Fort Davis. He glanced down as small fingers slipped into his.

"We are friends, aren't we, pretty man?"

Skye Fargo laughed.

LOOKING FORWARD!
The following is the opening section from the next novel in the exciting *Trailsman* series from Signet:

THE TRAILSMAN #329
BAYOU TRACKDOWN

The Louisiana swamp, 1861—where death came in many guises and many sizes.

The night was moonless but the mother wasn't worried.

Emmeline had been born and bred in the Atchafalaya Swamp. She knew the bayous and cypress haunts as city women knew streets and alleys. She was at home here.

So it was that on a hot, muggy summer night, Emmeline and her youngest, Halette, started out from the settlement for their cabin. The trails were as familiar to her as garden paths to a Southern belle. Emmeline thought nothing of the fact that the swamp crawled with snakes and alligators. She had her rifle and she was a good shot.

But as they were leaving her best friend's shack, Simone took her aside. "Maybe you should stay the night, *oui*? Start back in the morning fresh and rested."

"Non," Emmeline said. "We can be home in a couple of hours if we don't stop to rest too often."

"Your daughter is only eight. You expect too much of her," Simone criticized.

"No more than I expected of myself at her age." Emmeline kissed Simone on the cheek. "Don't worry. We'll be fine. I've done this countless times, have I not?"

"Even so," Simone said, and, glancing at Halette, she lowered her voice. "There have been stories."

"Oh, please."

"You've heard them. About the people who have gone missing. About a creature that is never seen but only heard. About the blood and the bones." Simone shuddered. "I tell you, they terrify me."

"Oh, please," Emmeline said again. "Am I a child to be made timid by horror tales?"

Emmeline and little Halette had been hiking under the stars for over an hour now. They were deep in the swamp, well past the last of the isolated cabins that dotted the watery domain of the cottonmouth, save one—their own cabin. And they still had a long way to go.

"I'm tired, *mère*," Halette remarked. She had her mother's oval face and fair complexion and her beautiful auburn hair.

"There is a spot ahead. It's not far. I suppose we can rest there for a few minutes."

"Merci."

The spot Emmeline was thinking of was a grassy hummock. The trail, after many twists and turns, often with water lapping at both sides, presently brought them there, and Halette, with a sigh of relief, sank down, curling her legs under her.

"Watch out for snakes," Emmeline cautioned.

"I'm too tired to care."

The breeze was strong. It brought with it the night sounds of the great swamp: the croak of frogs, the bellow of gators, the scream of a panther, and the shrieks of prey. These were sounds Emmeline was used to. She had heard them every night of her life. She gave them no more thought than a city woman would give the clatter of wagon wheels.

Emmeline sat down next to Halette, and her daughter leaned against her, saying quietly, "It's pretty out here."

"*Oui.* I have always loved the swamp. Many people are afraid of it, but to us, who live in it, it is part of us. It is in our blood and in our breath, and we can never be afraid."

"I am now and then. When I am in our cabin alone at night and I hear noises."

Emmeline squeezed Halette's shoulder. "That's normal, little one. When I was young as you, I would get scared, too. I imagined all sorts of things that were not real. Eventually you outgrow such silliness."

"I will try not to be afraid, for you."

Mother and daughter shared smiles, and the mother hugged the daughter, and it was then, from out of the benighted fastness of water and cypress and reeds, that there came a sound that caused the mother to stiffen and the daughter to gasp. It was a low rumbling, neither roar nor grunt yet a little of both, which rose to a piercing squeal and then abruptly stopped.

"What was that?" Halette exclaimed.

"I don't know," Emmeline admitted. "A gator, maybe."

"I never heard a gator do that. No bear, either. Yet it had to be something big. Really big."

"Whatever it was, it was far away."

"Was it? *Père* says that sometimes our ears play tricks on us. That what we think is far is close, and what we think is close is far."

Emmeline grinned and ruffled Halette's hair. "You worry too much. That is your problem." She rose. "Come. We should keep going. I do not want to take all night getting home."

They walked on, the mother holding the girl's hand, and if the girl walked so close that their hips brushed, the mother didn't say anything. They had gone several hundred feet and were in a belt of rank vegetation with solid ground all around when the strange sound was repeated. They both stopped.

"It's closer," Halette said.

"But still a ways off." Emmeline walked faster and was comforted by the old Sharps in the crook of her elbow. It held only one shot but it was powerful enough to bring down anything in the swamp. And she could hit a knothole in a tree at thirty paces.

"Wouldn't it be nice to sing?" Halette asked. "I like it when we sing."

So they sang, a new ditty popular with children called "The Pig Song" by a man named Burnand.

"There was a fiddler and he wore a wig. Wiggy, wiggy, wiggy, wiggy, weedle, weedle, weedle. He saved up his money and he bought a pig. Tweedle, tweedle, tweedle, tweedle, tweedle, tweedle, tweedle."

They were about to begin the second stanza when a rumbling grunt from out of the thick undergrowth brought them to a stop. Halette's fingernails dug so deep into Emmeline's palm they almost drew blood.

"It's really close, *mère*."

"Don't worry. I have my rifle." But Emmeline was worried herself. She thought it might be a black bear, and if so, it had to be a big one and the big ones were hard to kill. A single shot to the brain or the heart was not always enough. She walked faster.

Somewhere off in the darkness a twig snapped.

"I don't like this," Halette said.

"Be brave. I'm right here." But inside Emmeline, a swarm of butterflies was loose in her stomach. Or was it moths, since it was nighttime? She smiled at her humor, and then lost the smile when something crunched off in the trees.

"Did you hear that?"

"Stay calm. It might be a deer."

"No deer made that sound we heard," Halette insisted. "Whatever it is, it's following us."

"That's preposterous." But Emmeline had the same suspicion. She shifted her rifle so the muzzle was pointed at the side of the trail the thing was on.

"Should we climb a tree? *Père* says that's the best thing to do when a bear is after you."

"Only if it's a large bear," Emmeline amended. "Small bears can climb as well as we can."

The undergrowth rustled and crackled. They stopped, peered hard to try to spot the cause, and the crackling stopped. When they moved on, the crackling began again.

"What *is* it, *mère*?" Halette asked in stark fear.

"Stay calm," Emmeline said again. But deep inside she was just as scared. Whatever the thing was, it wasn't afraid of them. It was indeed stalking them and it didn't care if they knew it. Her palms grew slick with sweat and her mouth became dry.

For minutes that seemed like hours the taut tableau continued. Mother and daughter were glued to each other. Now and then the creature in the undergrowth grunted or snorted and the mother felt her youngest quake.

"I wish *père* was here," the girl said, not once but several times.

The mother thought of their cabin, so near and yet so far, and her husband, and she felt a burning sensation in the pit of her stomach that brought bitter bile to her mouth. She swallowed the bile back down.

Simone had been right to take the tales seriously, and Emmeline had been wrong. Those people who vanished—they hadn't become lost or fallen to the Mad Indian or run into Remy Cuvier's cutthroats. Not that Remy would ever harm her, or any other Cajun, for that matter. The thing in the woods was to blame. She knew that as surely as she knew anything.

Then the growth thinned and ahead lay a stretch of swamp where the trail was no wider than a broad man's shoulders. Water lapped the edges. Here and there hummocks of land choked with growth broke the surface.

Emmeline's heart leaped in fragile hope. The thing could not get at them now without her seeing it. She would be able to get off a shot, and must make the shot count. Emboldened, she said for her daughter's benefit, "Let that animal show itself now and I will put a hole in its head."

Halette laughed a short, nervous laugh.

They redoubled their speed. A city girl using that serpentine trail in the dark of night would inch along like a turtle, but Emmeline and Halette were bayou born and bred, and to them a trail three feet wide was as good as a road. They covered a hundred yards, and there was no sign of the creature. Two hundred yards, and the only sounds were those of the insects, frogs and gators, a familiar chorus that soothed their troubled hearts.

"I guess it was nothing," Halette broke their silence, and laughed again.

No sooner were the words out of her young mouth than a loud splash warned them that something large was in the water.

"A gator," Emmeline said.

"Sure," Halette agreed.

But then the thing that made the splash grunted, and icy cold fear rippled down their spines.

"It's still following us!" Halette gasped.

"Perhaps it is something harmless." But Emmeline didn't believe that. Her fright was heightened by the thought that whatever that thing was, it must know about guns. How else to explain why it moved away from them when they came to the open water, yet still shadowed them?

"If only our cabin wasn't so far."

"We'll make it," Emmeline said, and patted Halette on the head. "I won't ever let anything happen to you."

"Frogs eat bugs and snakes eat frogs and gators eat snakes and frogs and people, too," Halette said softly.

It was a family saying. It stemmed from when their oldest, Clovis, was younger than Halette, and they were trying to make him understand that while the bayous and swamps were places of great beauty, they were also places of great danger. To a five-year-old boy, the world was a friend. It took some doing for Emmeline and Namo to convince Clovis that he must be wary of the many creatures that could do him harm. To that end, Emmeline came up with a rhyme to remind him. Silly, but it helped, and Clovis came to see that while the world was his friend, some of the creatures he shared the world with weren't friendly.

"Listen!" Halette exclaimed.

The thing was grunting and snorting in a frenzy, and the splashing had grown so loud, the very swamp seemed to be in upheaval.

"It's fighting something!"

Emmeline thought so, too. A gator, perhaps. Or one of the huge snakes, rare but spotted from time to time by the human denizens of the great swamp. Town and city dwellers scoffed at the notion, saying snakes never grew to thirty meters or more and were never as thick around as large trees. But the swamp dwellers saw with their own eyes, and knew the truth.

There were other tales, too. Of things only talked about behind locked doors in the flickering glow of candles. Of goblins and ghosts and three-toed skunk apes. But Emmeline never believed in any of that. Her Namo did. He was as superstitious as a person could be, but he was a good provider and a good husband, so she put up with his charms and bones and rabbit's feet.

The splashing and grunting ended in a high-pitched squeal that climbed to an ear-piercing shriek.

Halette said, "Something is dying."

Emmeline went rigid with shock. She almost told her daughter that no, that wasn't it. The squeal wasn't the death cry of the loser; it was the cry of triumph of the victor. At last she realized what it was, and fear filled every fiber of her being. "Run," she said.

And they ran.

A hundred feet more would bring them to a hummock, and trees. Those trees, Emmeline hoped, would prove their salvation. She held her daughter's hand firmly and the two of them fairly flew. She could go faster, but Halette was at her limit.

"Mère!"

Emmeline had heard. The splashing was coming toward them. The thing had decided to end the cat and mouse and was making a beeline for them. They must reach the trees or they were doomed.

Suddenly the hummock appeared, a low mound bisected by the trail. The trees were not many but some had thick trunks and might resist being uprooted. Emmeline raced to one, hooked her hands under Halette's arms, and practically heaved her at the lowest limbs, shouting, "Grab hold and climb!"

"What about you?"

Emmeline whirled. The massive monster was almost on top of them. She jerked her rifle to her shoulder and took aim. But even as she fired, and her daughter screamed, Emmeline knew these were her last moments on earth. Her rifle boomed but it had no effect, and then the thing was on her. Emmeline tried to be brave—she tried not to scream—but God, the pain, the searing, awful, ripping and rending.

It seemed to go on forever.